MICHAEL KOHLHAAS

Heinrich von Kleist

MICHAEL KOHLHAAS

translated from the German
by Michael Hofmann

A NEW DIRECTIONS PAPERBOOK

First published as New Directions Paperbook 1473 in 2020
Manufactured in the United States of America
New Directions Books are printed on acid-free paper
Design by Erik Rieselbach

Library of Congress Cataloging-in-Publication Data
Names: Kleist, Heinrich von, 1777–1811, author. | Hofmann, Michael, translator.
Title: Michael Kohlhaas / by Heinrich von Kleist ; translated by Michael Hofmann.
Other titles: Michael Kohlhaas. English
Description: New York, New York : A New Directions Book, 2020. |
Originally published in Germany in 1810. | Translated from the German.
Identifiers: LCCN 2019053988 |
ISBN 9780811228343 (paperback ; acid-free paper) |
ISBN 9780811228350 (ebook)
Classification: LCC PT2378.M62 H64 2020 | DDC 833/.6—dc23
LC record available at https://lccn.loc.gov/2019053988

2 4 6 8 10 9 7 5 3 1

New Directions Books are published for James Laughlin
by New Directions Publishing Corporation
80 Eighth Avenue, New York 10011

MICHAEL KOHLHAAS

In the middle of the 16th century there lived on the banks of the Havel a horse dealer by the name of Michael Kohlhaas, son of a schoolmaster, at once one of the most righteous and appalling individuals of his time. Until his thirtieth year, this unusual man would have been accounted the very model of a good citizen. In the village that still bears his name, he owned a farm that provided him with a comfortable living; the children his wife gave him he brought up in the fear of God, to be hardworking and loyal; there was not one among his neighbors who hadn't benefited from his charity and his fair dealing; in sum, the world would have blessed his memory, if he hadn't followed one of his virtues to excess. His sense of justice led him to robbery and murder.

Once, he left his home with a string of colts, all of them well-fed and with shining coats, and he was just thinking of what he would do with the profit he stood to realize from their sale at various markets—some of it, in the manner of prudent landlords, he would reinvest, but the rest he meant to use for his present enjoyment—when he came to the River Elbe and saw a stately castle on Saxon territory, along with a toll barrier he hadn't previously met with on this route. At a moment when the rain was teeming down, he stopped with his horses and called out to the tollkeeper, who soon after stuck his sour-looking face out at a window. The horse dealer asked to be allowed to pass. What have we here? he asked as the tollkeeper eventually stepped out of the hut. Royal privilege, came the reply, as he made to let him pass: licensed to the Junker Wenzel von Tronka.

I see, said Kohlhaas, the Junker's name is Wenzel? And he inspected the gleaming battlements of the castle louring over the countryside. Is the old lord dead then?

Died of an apoplexy, replied the tollkeeper, pushing the barrier aside.

Hmm, I'm sorry to hear it, said Kohlhaas. He was a dignified old gentleman who liked to have people coming and going, assisted commerce in any way he could, and once, at his own expense, had the road improved where the track enters the village because one of my mares suffered a broken leg there. Well, now he's gone. And what do I owe? he asked, and with some difficulty he fished the coppers the tollkeeper demanded from under the skirts of his flapping coat. "Ah, the old man," he added, as the tollkeeper was saying, Make haste, make haste! and cursing the weather: "If yon tree had been permitted to stay in the forest, it would have been better for all of us," and he paid him the toll money, and was about to go on his way. No sooner had he passed the barrier, though, than another voice rang out, calling from the tower behind: Hold hard, horseman! and he saw the castellan slam shut a window, and hurry downstairs. What is it now? Kohlhaas asked himself and reined in his horses. The castellan buttoning a jerkin over his capacious belly, asked, leaning into the wind, for his pass.

My pass? asked Kohlhaas. A little crestfallen, he said that

to the best of his knowledge he had none; but if he were told what manner of thing this was, then he would certainly do his best to kit himself out with one. The castellan gave him a sidelong look and said that without a permit from the local lord, no trader with horses was permitted to cross the frontier. The horse dealer assured him he had passed this frontier seventeen times in the course of his life without any such document; that he was well-acquainted with all the official stipulations concerning his business; that this was surely a mistake, and he asked him to reconsider, begging him, since his day's journey was arduous, not to detain him any longer without reason. But the castellan replied that he wasn't about to let him slip through for an eighteenth time, that this was a decree that had newly been promulgated, and that he would either have to acquire a pass on the spot or be forced to turn back. The horse dealer, beginning to find these arbitrary constraints irksome, after a brief pause for thought got off his horse, left it with a squire, and said he would take up the matter with this Tronka in person. He went up into the castle, the castellan following him all the while muttering darkly about sharp practice and salutary bleeding; and both entered the room together, eyeing one another. It transpired that the Junker was sitting over wine with a few of his associates, and a great peal of laughter over some pleasantry was just ringing out as Kohlhaas advanced to make his complaint. The Junker asked him what his business was; his friends, seeing the stranger, fell silent, but no sooner had he begun his plea regarding the horses than the whole group almost as one, called out: Horses? Where? and hurried over to the window to look. Seeing the gleaming backs, at a suggestion of the Junker, they hurried down into the courtyard; the rain in the meantime had stopped; and castellan and steward and squires all assembled and appraised the animals. One liked the sorrel with the blazon on his brow, a second the chestnut, a third stroked the brindle with the black and yellow patches; all of them were agreed that the horses were as spirited as stags, and that in all the land there were none better. Kohlhaas happily replied that the horses were no better than those who would ride them and urged them to make a purchase. The Junker, who was greatly drawn to the powerful sorrel, asked him what his price was; his steward urged him to buy a couple of the horses, that he had good use for in the running of the estate, which was short of mounts, but when the dealer named his price, the knights found it too steep, and the Junker said he would have to ride to the Round Table and borrow from King Arthur himself if he had such a price in mind. In some dark presentiment and seeing the castellan and the steward exchanging glances and whispers, Kohlhaas made every effort nonetheless to sell the horses. He said to the Junker: "Sir, I bought these black mares for twenty-five gold ducats not six months ago; give me thirty, and they are yours." Two of the knights, standing by the Junker, expressed themselves to the effect that the horses were surely worth such a sum; but the Junker reckoned that he would spend money on the sorrel, but not on the others, and made to leave; whereupon Kohlhaas said perhaps they might reach an agreement the next time he came through; said goodbye to the Junker, and took the bridle of his horse to ride off. At that moment the castellan emerged from the ruck and said: Mark him, he was not allowed to leave without a pass. Kohlhaas turned and asked the Junker if this was indeed the case, because if so, it meant the ruination of his business. Himself turning to leave, the Junker said with a sheepish expression: Yes, Kohlhaas, you must buy a pass. Talk to the castellan and go your ways. Kohlhaas assured him he had no intention of avoiding the rules that applied to the export of horses; he promised to obtain a pass in the government notariat on his way through Dresden and asked him just this once—seeing as he was so entirely unprepared for this demand—to let him pass. Well, said the Junker, as the weather just again began to turn nasty, and the wind blew through his thin limbs, let the lucky chancer go. Come, he said to his retinue, and turned to go back inside. Facing the Junker, the castellan said the fellow should at least be required to leave some warranty that he would indeed obtain the permit. The Junker stopped in the gateway. Kohlhaas asked what value, in money or objects, he should leave behind to guarantee his black mares? The steward reckoned, muttering into his beard, that he might as well leave the mares themselves. That's true, said the castellan, that would be the most practical solution; once the permit has been obtained, he can come back and pick them up at his convenience. Kohlhaas, dismayed by such an insolent requirement, said to the Junker, who was clasping his tunic to try and stay warm, that his whole purpose was to take the horses to market; but the Junker, since at that instant a puff of wind chased a flurry of rain and hail through the gateway, called out to put an end to the affair: If he won't relinquish the horses, then toss him back across the barrier; and so left. The horse breeder, who could see he had no option but to yield to brute force decided to fulfill the other's demands; he untied the mares and led them to a stable to which the castellan took him. He left a groom behind with them, supplied him with money, instructed him to look after them until his return, and resumed his journey with the rest of the string to the noble city of Leipzig where he meant to attend the fair, half wondering whether, in view of a nascent Saxon trade in horses, such a restrictive measure might not indeed have been passed there.

Straight after his arrival in Dresden, where he owned a property on the outskirts of the town, with stabling for a few horses, that he used as a base for his tours to the other smaller fairs in the land, he betook himself to the government notariat, where the notaries, some of whom he knew, confirmed what instinct had already told him: namely that the story of a pass was a fairytale. Kohlhaas, whom the sympathetic notaries at his insistence furnished with written confirmation that there was no basis in fact for the levy, smiled at the jest played by the bony Junker, even though he didn't really see what its purpose might be; and having sold the rest of his horses to his satisfaction in the ensuing weeks, he returned without any bitterness except at the general condition of the world, to Tronkenburg. The castellan, to whom he produced the certificate, made no comment, and to the breeder's question about the return of his horses, replied that he might go down and fetch them. Even as he was crossing the courtyard, Kohlhaas made the disagreeable discovery that his groom, for bad conduct, as was said, had been soundly beaten and chased away from Tronkenburg shortly after he had left him there. He asked the lad who told him the news what was it the groom had done? And who had looked after the horses since? To which the lad replied that he didn't know, and thereupon opened the stables in which they stood to the horse breeder, whose heart was already big with anxiety. How great nevertheless was his dismay that in place of his two sleek and well-fed sable mares, he saw a couple of shrunken bony creatures; ribs like barrel hoops; their manes and tails, without attention and grooming, all matted: the very picture of animal distress. Kohlhaas, to whom the beasts feebly whinnied, was dismayed in the extreme, and asked what had befallen his horses? The lad who was standing by him replied that it was no misfortune as such, they had been provided with proper feed too, but that as it had been harvest time, and there was a shortage of draft animals, they had been used for a little fieldwork. Kohlhaas swore at such shameful and conniving practice, but feeling his inability to do anything, stifled his fury, and as there was nothing for it, made to leave this nest of thieves with his horses, when the castellan, summoned by the sound of conversation, appeared and asked what was going on? What's going on? said Kohlhaas. Who gave Tronka and his people permission to use my mares I left with him for work in the harvest? Was such a thing human? he added, tried to rouse the exhausted horses by a stroke of the switch, and showed the castellan that they were incapable of stirring. After looking at him stonily for some time the castellan said: Behold the ruffian! Should the villain not instead praise God that his mares were still alive? Who, since the groom had run off, was supposed to look after them? Was it not fair exchange that the feed they were given should have been earned from their labor? He finished by saying he wasn't to kick up a fuss, otherwise he would call the dogs on him, and they would see to it that there was quiet again.

The horse breeder could feel his heart thumping under his tunic. He felt an urge to dump the fat-bellied ne'er-do-well in the filth and grind his heel in those ruddy features. But his sense of justice, which was as finely equilibrated as a pair of jeweler's scales, was still trembling in the balance; outside the tribunal of his own bosom he could not be sure whether some guilt was oppressing the other party or not; and, swallowing back fresh tirades of his own, he stepped over to the horses, and in quiet contemplation stroking their manes, he asked in a soft voice: For what misconduct was his groom ejected from the castle? The castellan replied: Because the rascal was impertinent on the estate! Because he tried to stand in the way of a necessary move to another stable and demanded that the mounts of two young gentlemen who were visiting Tronkenburg spend the night on the open road, in place of his own two mares!

Kohlhaas would happily have shelled out the price of the two horses to have had his groom present, to compare his witness to the statement of the loudmouthed castellan. He was still standing there, teasing the knots out of the horses' manes, and thinking what to do when the scene abruptly changed, and Junker Wenzel von Tronka with a rout of knights, grooms, and dogs came clattering into the courtyard, fresh from a chase of hares. The castellan, asked what the matter was, straightaway spoke up, and while the dogs, sighting the stranger, from one side set up a bloodthirsty baying, and the knights, from the other did their best to hish them, he claimed, with egregious misrepresentation of the facts, that the horse breeder was peeved because his horses had been put to work a little. He said, to scornful laughter, that the man refused to acknowledge the horses were even his. Kohlhaas called out: "No, indeed, they are not my horses, if it please your honor! These are not the horses that were worth thirty gold ducats! I want the return of my sleek and well-fed horses!"

The Junker, across whose face a fleeting pallor was seen to pass, dismounted and declared if the wretch doesn't want his horses, let him leave them here. Günther! he called, Hans! Come! Brushing the dust from his garments and calling: Bring wine! he entered the castle, and then he and the knights were all within. Kohlhaas said he would sooner call the knacker and have the horses sold for glue than take them back to Kohlhaasenbrück in their present condition. Without further ado he left the horses where they were, swung himself up in the saddle of his chestnut, and assuring anyone who cared to hear that he knew how to obtain his rights, rode off.

He was on the best way to Dresden, when, thinking of his groom, and the grievance they had against him at the castle, he slowed to a walk, and finally before he had gone a thousand steps, turned his horse, and made instead for Kohlhaasenbrück to question his groom, as now seemed both urgent and prudent. His instinct, already well-acquainted with the infirm constitution of the world, inclined him—in spite of the insults he had suffered, and if it really was the case, that, as the castellan claimed, the groom was guilty of some transgression—to accept the loss of the horses as nothing more than he deserved. Countering this was another feeling, just as distinct, which took ever deeper root within him, that, as he rode on, making the occasional stops, and hearing everywhere of the injustices that were daily practiced on travelers at Tronkenburg: that if the whole incident, as seemed to be the case, was a conspiracy, he with all his strength was duty bound to obtain satisfaction for the insult he had suffered, and security for future citizens.

No sooner had he arrived in Kohlhaasenbrück and embraced Lisbeth his dear wife, and kissed his children, who gleefully clustered round him, than he straightaway asked after Herse, his groom: had nothing been heard from him? Lisbeth said: Oh, my dear Michael, Herse! Imagine, this unhappy man, beaten most piteously, arrives here two weeks ago: So badly beaten he can hardly draw breath. We put him to bed where he spits blood and, in answer to our repeated questions, are regaled with a story that none of us can make any sense of. How he had been left behind at Tronkenburg with the horses that had not been permitted passage, how by the most injurious mistreatment he had been forced to leave the castle, and how he had been prevented from taking the horses with him. Oh? said Kohlhaas, taking off his cloak. And is he any better now?

Apart from the spitting blood, she said, a little. I wanted to send another groom to Tronkenburg right away to see to the horses till your return. Because since Herse has always shown himself to be an honest and faithful servant as no other, it didn't feel right to me to question his statement, for which there was so much support, for instance to think that he might have lost the horses in some other way. But he beseeches me not to allow anyone else to set foot in this nest of thieves, and to give up the animals if I am not to sacrifice any other man for them.

Is he in bed still? asked Kohlhaas, taking off his neckcloth.

He has been up now for the past few days, she replied. But you will see, she continued, that everything is as he says, and that this event is one of the pranks that they have indulged in against strangers of late in Tronkenburg.

I will look into the matter, replied Kohlhaas. Call him for me, Lisbeth, if he's up, let him come to me. With these words, he took to his chair; and the woman of the house, rejoicing in his steady demeanor, went out and fetched the groom.

Now then, what did you get up to in Tronkenburg? asked Kohlhaas, as Lisbeth entered the room with him. I am most displeased with you.

The groom, on whose pallid face a few splotches of red showed at these words, was silent for a time, then replied: Sir, you are right. Because I took a sulfur string that I happened to be carrying with me to set fire to the nest of thieves I had been driven out of, but then when I heard a child crying within, I threw it instead in the river, and thought: May God incinerate it with one of His lightnings, I won't!

Kohlhaas said strickenly: But what did you do to deserve being dismissed from Tronkenburg? Whereto Herse: They played me false, sir, and mopped the sweat from his brow, but what's done is done. I didn't want the horses to be ruined by field work, and said they were still young and unused to pulling.

Kohlhaas countered, trying to conceal his bewilderment, that this wasn't quite the truth, at the beginning of the past spring, they had both been put in harness for a little while. You should, he continued, as a sort of guest at the castle, have shown willing on one or more occasions, not least if they were anxious to bring in the harvest.

And so I did, sir, replied Herse. I thought, looking at their dour expressions, it won't be the end of the horses. On the third morning, I put them in harness, and I brought in three loads of grain. Kohlhaas, whose heart was quaking, cast his eyes down, and said: I wasn't told of this, Herse!

Herse assured him this was indeed the case. My disobligingness, he said, consisted of refusing to harness up the horses at midday, the moment they had been fed and watered, and that when the castellan and the steward both put it to me that I might accept free feed from them, and keep the money you had entrusted me with to pay for their fodder, I replied that was the last thing I would do, and turned and left.

But it wasn't for that piece of disobligingness that you were turned away from Tronkenburg, said Kohlhaas.

Heaven forfend, said the groom, damnable mischief! For in the evening the horses of two young gentlemen who were arrived at Tronkenburg were led into the stable, and my two were made fast to the stable door. And when I took them from the hands of the castellan, who had moved them there, and asked where the animals would go now, he led me to a pigsty, a lean-to built of boards and laths against the wall of the castle.

You mean, Kohlhaas now interrupted him, you mean it was so lamentably ill-suited for horses that it was more like a sty than a stable.

Sir, it was a pigsty, replied Herse. A veritable pigsty, with pigs going in and out of it, and so low I couldn't stand upright in it.

Perhaps there was no other shelter available, suggested Kohlhaas; the visitors' horses took precedence, one can understand that.

Stable room, replied the groom, lowering his voice, was indeed scarce. There were now seven knights staying in the castle, all told. If it had been you, you would have suggested moving the horses together a little. I said I would try and find stabling in the village; but the castellan objected that he had to keep the horses under his personal observation, and that I was on no account to try and take them out of the yard.

Hm! said Kohlhaas. And what did you say to that?

Because the steward said two of the guests were only staying one night, and would be leaving in the morning, I took the horses and put them in the pigsty. But the next day came and went without any change; and on the morning of the third day, I was told the gentlemen would be staying several weeks longer.

I think, Herse, it won't have been so bad in the pigsty as it seemed to you the instant you first stuck your nose in there.

True, true, replied the groom. Once I'd swept the place, it improved. I gave the maid a piece of money to take the pigs somewhere else. And over the day I thought of a way for the horses to stay upright, by lifting the laths off the beams when it got light and putting them back at night. So now, like geese, they stuck their heads up through the roof, and gazed in the direction of Kohlhaasenbrück or wherever else things were pleasanter.

I see, asked Kohlhaas, so why in the world did they drive you away?

I'll tell you, sir, said the groom. It's because they wanted to be rid of me. Because for as long as I was there, they were unable to grind the horses into destruction. Everywhere I went in the yard and in the servants' room, they greeted me with foul grimaces; and because I thought, go on, pull your faces till they break, they manufactured an occasion, and they threw me out.

But what was the occasion! cried Kohlhaas. They will have had some cause.

O indeed they did, replied Herse, and it was the justest cause imaginable. On the evening of our second day in the pigsty, I took out the horses, which were all befouled, to ride them down to the Mulde. And just as I was passing under the main gate, to turn down to the river, I hear the castellan and the steward, with dogs and whips and grooms from the servants' quarters chasing after me, crying: Stop the villain! Rascal, stop! as if they were mad. The tollkeeper came out to meet me; and when I ask him and the crazed rabble who are coming after me: What's the matter? What is it? The castellan replies; and takes my horse by the bridle. Where are you going with those horses, he asks, and takes me by the scruff. I say, Where am I going? Good God! I'm riding down to the river. You don't suppose I'm—? The river? cries the castellan. You rascal, I'll have you swim back to Kohlhaasenbrück! And with a sudden murderous move, he and the steward who took my leg, they throw me off the horse, so that I measure my full length in the mud. Murder! I cry, Help! My ropes and blankets and a pile of linen are all back in the stables; but while the steward leads the horses away, the castellan and the grooms, with kicks and punches and blows from whips and cudgels lay into me, till I'm lying half dead behind the gateway. And as I say: The robber dogs! Where are they taking my horses? And get to my feet. Off the premises, screams the castellan, and: Ho, Kaiser, ho, Jäger, I hear, and ho, Spitz! And at least a dozen dogs come flying at me. Then I break off a plank of wood, I don't really know, from the fence, and I strike three of the dogs dead, but finally, crippled by agonizing bites I have to yield: Toot! a whistle sounds; the dogs retreat into the yard, the wings of the gate are shut, the bolt is pushed across: and I collapse unconscious in the street.

With forced humor, though pale in the face, Kohlhaas remarked: And are you sure you weren't thinking of escaping somewhere, Herse? And when Herse, blushing darkly, looked down: Admit it, he said, you weren't happy in your pigsty; you preferred the stable in Kohlhaasenbrück after all.

Good Christ! called Herse. I left saddlery and blankets and a bundle of linens back in the pigsty. And wouldn't I have stopped to pocket the three guineas that I had hidden in a red silk neckerchief behind the hay crib? Thunder, damn, and devil! To hear you talk like that puts me in a mood to relight the sulfur thread I threw away. Now, now! said the horse breeder, you know I meant no harm. Listen, I believe every word of your account as though it were gospel. I'm sorry you fared no better in my service; now go, Herse, go to bed, have them bring you a bottle of wine, and take comfort. You will have justice. And with that he stood up, made an inventory of the items the groom left behind in the pigsty; attached a value to them, asked him how much he thought his medical attention had cost; and having shaken him once more by the hand, allowed him to leave.

Thereupon he told his wife Lisbeth all that had happened and its wider impact, explaining how determined he was to secure justice for himself in the courts, and was delighted to see that she fully stood by him in his resolve. For she said there were other travelers too, perhaps less easygoing than he was, who would visit the castle; that it would be a good work to put a stop to injustices like this; and that she would set about bringing in the costs that such a case would occasion. Kohlhaas called her his good, loyal wife, enjoyed the day and the day after in her company and that of their children, and as soon as his business permitted, he set off to Dresden to bring his case to court.

There, with the help of a lawyer of his acquaintance, he composed a complaint in which, following a detailed account of the crimes perpetrated against himself and his groom Herse by the Junker Wenzel von Tronka, he demanded lawful punishment of the latter, the restoration of the horses in their original state, and payment of such damages as he and his groom had suffered. The case was clear in law. The circumstance that the horses had been unlawfully detained cast a clear light on all subsequent matters; and even if one had supposed they had become ill or infirm by chance, the horse breeder's demand that they be restored to him in good health would still have been unarguable. Nor did Kohlhaas, as he was looking about him in the city, find himself short of friends who seemed likely to lend vigorous support to his cause; his long-established trade in horses had got him the acquaintance, and the honesty with which he pursued it the favor of some of the most important men in the state. Several times he dined gaily with his lawyer, who was himself a well-respected man; he deposited with him a sum of money for the conduct of the case; and at the end of a few weeks, completely assured by him as to their prospects, he returned to his wife Lisbeth in Kohlhaasenbrück. Months went by, and the year was almost up before he heard there was any progress of the case in Saxony, much less its resolution. After the case had stalled several times, he asked in a confidential letter to his attorney what it was that was causing such an excessive delay; and learned that following some discreet intervention from some well-placed party at the Dresden Court it had been quashed.

To the uncomprehending reply of the trader what the cause of this might be, he received the following answer: That Wenzel von Tronka had two cousins, Hinz and Kunz von Tronka, of whom one was the cupbearer to the Elector, and the other his Chamberlain.

He urged him to set aside the case, and merely seek to take back the horses that were still at Tronkenburg; giving him to understand that the Junker, who was currently in the city himself, seemed to have left instructions with his staff to deliver them up to him; and he ended by asking him, if he wasn't minded to cry enough at this point, at least not to trouble him, the lawyer, with any further instructions in the matter.

Kohlhaas happened just then to be in Brandenburg, where the Lord Mayor, Heinrich von Geusau, whose district included Kohlhaasenbrück, was busy setting up several charitable institutions for the sick and the poor, from a sizable legacy that had been left to the city. In particular, he was at pains to develop a stream in one of the local villages, of whose health-giving properties people made more than turned out to be the case, for the use of invalids; and knowing Kohlhaas from the time they both had been at Court, he gave permission for Herse, the groom, who ever since his awful sojourn at Tronkenburg had drawn no breath without pain, to try the effectiveness of the waters, which had by now been fitted out with a roof and a tap. It turned out that the Mayor was present beside the font at which Kohlhaas had left Herse, to deliver some instructions, just as he, reached by an envoy sent after him by his wife, received the crushing news from his advocate in Dresden. The Mayor, as he was speaking to one of the doctors, noticing that a tear fell from Kohlhaas's eye onto the letter he had received, now approached him in a sympathetic manner, and asked him what mischance had occurred; and when the trader, without a word, passed him the letter, then the worthy gentleman, familiar with the appalling injustice he had incurred at Tronkenburg—part of the consequence of which was Herse's condition, which might persist for the rest of his life—patted him on the back and said: He should take courage, he would help him obtain satisfaction. That evening, when the horse breeder in accordance with his instructions had gone up to see him in the castle, he told him he had merely to address a petition, with a brief account of the incident, to the Elector of Brandenburg, enclose the letter from the lawyer, and ask for protection from the overlord of the country on account of the violence he had suffered on Saxon terrain. He promised he would put the petition, along with another parcel that was waiting to be delivered into the hands of the Elector of Brandenburg, who could then, if circumstances allowed, be relied upon to take influence on the Elector of Saxony; and such a step would be sufficient to see that justice was done, in spite of all at the court of Dresden and the machinations of the Junker and his mob. Highly delighted, Kohlhaas sincerely thanked the Mayor for this new proof of his attachment; said he was only sorry that he could not have his matter seen to there and then in Berlin, without involving Dresden again; and after drawing up his complaint in the city's chancellery department in accordance with the Mayor's instructions, and handing it to him, he returned, more sanguine than ever as to the outcome of his affair, to Kohlhaasenbrück. Only a few weeks later, then, he was upset to hear from a legal gentleman traveling to Potsdam on the affairs of the Mayor, that the Elector had handed the petition to his minister, Count Kallheim, and that this gentleman had not immediately, as seemed appropriate, set about investigating and punishing the violence at the Court in Dresden, but had applied to Tronka for further information. The legal gentleman who, stopping in his carriage outside Kohlhaas's apartments, seemed to be under instruction to convey such information to the horse breeder, was unable to find a satisfactory answer to his question: What do we do now? He merely added: The Mayor urged him to be patient; he appeared in a hurry to get on with his journey; and only at the end of this brief meeting did Kohlhaas guess from some stray words that Count Kallheim was a relation by marriage of the Tronkas.

Kohlhaas, taking no pleasure in anything anymore, not in his horses, not in house and yard, and barely in wife and children, full of foreboding as to what might happen next, waited out the rest of the month; and then, as he had expected, Herse returned from Brandenburg, slightly improved from the waters, with a note from the Mayor accompanying a lengthier official document, to the effect that he was sorry he was unable to accomplish anything in his matter; he was sending him a judgment he had received from the Chancellery, and urged him to take back the horses that had been left behind in Tronkenburg, and otherwise to let the matter rest.

The judgment went: "It is the view of the Dresden court that he is a chronic complainant; the Junker with whom he left his horses is in no wise keeping them from him; let him send to the castle and collect them, or at the very least let the Junker know where he should send them; but he should desist from bothering the Court with his moans and gripes." Kohlhaas, whose prime interest was not the horses—he would have felt as much pain had they been a couple of dogs—boiled with rage when he received the missive. Each time there was a sound in the yard he looked out with an expression of the most disgusted apprehension in the direction of the road to see if it was not the Junker's servants, come, perhaps even with an apology, to return the starved and exhausted horses; the only known occasion when his spirit, hitherto well-treated by the world, was braced for an outcome that did not accord with its natural serenity. Shortly after, he heard from an acquaintance who had traveled along that road that the Tronkenburg horses were being used, as before, like the rest of the Junker's horses, for field work; and in the midst of his pain to see the world in such disarray, an inner contentment twitched to see his own instincts at least in order. He invited a neighboring magistrate, who for a long time had thought to extend his property by acquiring his neighbor's possessions, and, once he had sat down, asked the magistrate what he would offer for his holdings in Brandenburg and Saxony, all of them, goods and chattels. Lisbeth, his wife, turned pale when she heard him. She turned away and picked up her youngest who was playing behind her on the floor, darting deathly expressions past the bonny cheeks of the boy toying with her ribbons at the horse breeder and at the paper he was holding in his hand. The magistrate looked at Kohlhaas in astonishment, and asked what prompted such an extraordinary move; whereupon his host, with as much levity as he could muster, replied: The thought of selling his farm on the banks of the Havel wasn't new to him; they had both spoken many times about a possible sale; his house outside Dresden was, by comparison, a mere bauble, inconsiderable; and to put it briefly, if he would do him the favor of taking both properties off his hands, he was prepared to set his name to a bill of sale. With forced pleasantry, he added that there was more to the world than Kohlhaasenbrück; and there might be certain purposes compared to which his domestic role as father and head of household dwindled into insignificance; in a word, that his mind had before it a great objective, of which the other might come to hear before long. The magistrate, somewhat relieved at these words, said, in a droll manner to the wife who was frenziedly kissing her baby: Surely he wouldn't require immediate payment? And he laid his hat and stick which he had held between his knees on the table and picked up the sheet of paper that the horse breeder held in his hand to peruse it. Kohlhaas, moving nearer, explained that this was a contract of sale which would be voided after four weeks; there was nothing missing from it save only their two signatures and the stipulation of a sum, being the price of the sale, and also the compensation he stood to receive should Kohlhaas resile from the contract within four weeks; and he invited him to sign, assuring him that he was willing, and would make no great difficulties. The good wife meanwhile walked up and down the room; her bosom was heaving, such that the kerchief with which her infant was playing threatened to slip off her shoulder altogether. The magistrate declared that he was in no position to assess the value of the Dresden property; whereupon Kohlhaas, pushing across to him correspondence from the time of its acquisition, replied: That he assessed it at one hundred gold gulden; even though it was shown that it had cost at least half as much again. The landowner, perusing the contract a second time, including the unusual freedom it gave him of withdrawing from the purchase, said, his mind already half made up: that he had no use for the mares that were at present in the stables; but when Kohlhaas replied that he had no intention of including them in the sale anyway, and that he also would like to keep a few of the weapons that were in the armory, so—he hesitated and hesitated, and finally repeated an offer that he had once made him, half in jest, half in earnest, in the course of a walk together, quite inadequate to the value of the property. Kohlhaas pushed pen and ink across to him to write it down; and when the magistrate, not believing his senses, asked him, was he serious, and the horse dealer a little irritably replied: Did he think he was playing? then, with a pensive expression, he picked up the pen and wrote; he crossed out the clause that stipulated that the deposit was forfeit if the vendor thought better of the sale; agreed to pay a mortgage of one hundred golden gulden on the title of the Dresden property which he had no interest in acquiring; and left the vendor two months of complete freedom to withdraw from the contract. The horse dealer, moved by his action, shook him warmly by the hand; and after they had agreed a principal condition, that one fourth of the price was to be paid immediately and in gold, and the remainder deposited with a bank in Hamburg in three months, he called for wine to toast the successful negotiation. He told the maid coming in with the bottles to tell Sternbald the groom to saddle the bay; he was riding to the capital on business; and he gave it to understand that shortly, on his return, he would talk more freely about matters he had still to keep for himself. Hereupon, as he filled their glasses, he asked about the Poles and Turks who were currently warring; involved the magistrate in various political debate on the subject; and once more toasted the success of their transaction and allowed him to leave.

Once the magistrate had left, Lisbeth fell to her knees in front of her husband. If you have any feeling in your heart for me, she cried, and for the children I have borne you; if we are not already, I know not why, cast out: then tell me what these awful preparations portend. Kohlhaas said: My darling wife, nothing that, as things stand, should cause you any disquiet. I received a copy of a judgment that says my suit against the Junker Wenzel von Tronka is a baseless fuss. And because that can only be a misunderstanding, I have taken it into my head to deliver my complaint in person to the Sovereign.

Why then sell the house? she cried, getting up, her features contorted with fear. The horse dealer, pressing her gently to his breast, replied: Because, my dear Lisbeth, I am not minded to live in a land in which my rights are not protected. Sooner to be a dog, if I am to be kicked, than a human being! I am convinced my wife will share my views.

And what makes you so certain that you will not be shielded in your rights, she asked wildly. If you approach our Sovereign modestly as befits you with your petition, how do you know it will be cast aside, or that they will refuse to give you a hearing?

Very well, replied Kohlhaas, if my fear proves groundless, then my house is not yet sold either. The Elector, I happen to know personally, is a just man; and if I succeed in cutting through his circle to the man himself, then I have no doubt I will obtain justice, and before the week is up, I will return to you happily, and to my old business. And then, he added, kissing her, there's nothing I should like better than to live gently with you till the end of my days!

But what is advisable, he went on, is that I be prepared for any eventuality; and so I would like you, if possible to take the children to Schwerin, to your aunt, whom you've been wanting to visit for some time now, I know.

What? cried the wife. You want me to go to Schwerin? To take the children across the border, and go to my aunt in Schwerin? Shock left her speechless.

Absolutely, said Kohlhaas, and if possible, right away, so that I am not disturbed in the next steps I mean to take in my affair.

"O! Now I understand you!" she exclaimed. "You don't need anything anymore, except weapons and horses; anyone can help themselves to what's left!" And so saying she turned away, threw herself down into a chair, and wept.

Strickenly, Kohlhaas said: My darling Lisbeth, what is it? God has blessed me with wife and child and possessions; am

I today to wish for the first time that He hadn't?—He gently sat down beside her, who, blushing at his words, threw herself upon him.

Tell me, he said, brushing the hair back from her brow: What shall I do? Shall I give up my case? Shall I go to Tronkenburg and ask the Junker to return my horses, swing myself into the saddle and ride home to you?

Lisbeth did not dare say: Yes! Yes! Yes!—weeping, she shook her head, pulled him to her and kissed his neck with hot kisses. "Well then!" exclaimed Kohlhaas. "If you concede that I must have justice if I am to carry on in my business, then accord me the freedom I need to obtain it!" And so saying he stood up and said to the groom who reported that the bay was saddled and ready: he ordered both chestnuts to be harnessed the following morning to take his wife to Schwerin. Lisbeth said she had a proposal to make. She got to her feet, wiped her eyes, and asked him, now sitting at his desk, if he would give her the petition and allow her, in his stead, to go to Berlin and deliver it to the Elector. Much moved by this turn, Kohlhaas settled her in his lap and said: My darling wife, that is plainly not possible! The Sovereign is surrounded on all sides, so that anyone seeking to approach him risks many unpleasantnesses. Lisbeth countered that there were a thousand situations in which it was easier for a woman to get through to him than a man. Give me your petition, she asked again; if all you want is the certainty that it will reach his hands, then I give you my word: he shall have it. Kohlhaas, who had evidence of her courage and cleverness in the past, asked how she proposed to go about it, to which, looking abashedly down, she replied: the Elector's castellan, in former times, when he had been posted in Schwerin, had sued for her hand; the man was now married, and the father of children, nonetheless, she was not forgotten—and in a word he could safely leave it to her, out of this and many another factor that it would take too long to describe, to draw some advantage. Kohlhaas with great joy kissed her, said he accepted her proposal, told her that it was enough to enter the apartments of the castellan's wife to be sure of being presented to the Sovereign, handed her the petition, had the chestnut horses put to, and sent her off well-packed and provided for with Sternbald, his loyal groom.

But of all the unsuccessful steps he had taken in his cause, this expedition was perhaps the least successful. A few days later, Sternbald returned to the farm, on foot beside the carriage in which the wife lay stretched out with a dangerously crushed ribcage. Kohlhaas turned pale as he stepped up to the conveyance and was unable to learn anything coherent about the cause of the mishap. The castellan, he was told by his groom, had not been at home, so that the little party had been obliged to stay the night at an inn near the castle; Lisbeth had left the inn the following morning, instructing the groom to remain behind with the horses; and it wasn't until evening that she returned, and in her present condition. It appeared she had all too brazenly thrust herself at the person of the Sovereign, and without him being in any way to blame, but merely through the overzealousness of a guard, she had received a blow in the chest from the butt of a lance. At any rate, that was what was said by the servants who towards evening carried her, unconscious still, to the inn; she herself was hardly able to speak because of the blood spilling out of her mouth. The petition had been taken out of her hands subsequently by a knight. Sternbald said it had been his desire to get on a horse right away and bring him the news of this unhappy accident; but in spite of the representations of the doctor, she had insisted on being brought back to her husband in Kohlhaasenbrück without any prior notification. Kohlhaas now brought her, quite destroyed by the journey, to bed, where, with painful efforts to draw breath, she lived one or two more days. Vain attempts were made to restore her to consciousness, for clarification of what happened; she lay there, her eyes unmoving and sightless, incapable of replying. Only just before she died did consciousness briefly return. For when a Lutheran minister was standing at her bedside (following her husband's example, she had gone over to the newly spreading religion), and in solemn tones was reading out a chapter from scripture, she suddenly looked at him with a grim expression, took the Bible out of his hands, as though he was not to read to her from it, and seemed to look in it for something; then with her finger she showed Kohlhaas sitting at her bedside the following verse: "Forgive thine enemies; do good also to those that hate you."

Then with a soul-filled look she pressed his hand, and she died.

Kohlhaas thought: May God never forgive me as I mean to forgive the Junker! Tears pouring down his cheeks, he kissed her, thumbed shut her eyes, and left the chamber. He took the hundred gold gulden his neighbor had already paid him for his house in Dresden and ordered a funeral befitting a duchess: with an oak coffin, reinforced with metal, silken pillows with gold and silver tassels, and a grave eight ells deep, lined with field stones and chalk. He himself stood beside the pit, with his youngest in his arms, and watched the work. When the day came for the burial, the body, white as snow, was set up in a hall he had had lined with black linen. The minister had just finished a moving oration at her bier when the decision arrived from the Sovereign regarding the petition conveyed to him by the late departed, to the effect that he was to collect the horses from Tronkenburg and on pain of prison take no further steps in the matter. Kohlhaas pocketed the letter and had the coffin loaded onto a carriage. As soon as the mound had been made, and the cross planted in it, and the mourners were leaving, he threw himself down once more at her now vacated bedside, and then embarked on the business of revenge. He sat down and composed an ultimatum in which by the power vested in him he ordered Junker Wenzel von Tronka, within three days of receipt to return to Kohlhaasenbrück the horses he had taken from him and ruined on his fields and personally feed them back to health. This document he sent with a mounted envoy, instructing him to return to Kohlhaasenbrück after its delivery. Since the three days had now elapsed without return of the horses, he summoned Herse; told him what he had ordered the young noble to do with respect to the feeding of the horses; and then he asked him two questions. Would he accompany him to Tronkenburg and collect the knight; and would he supervise him at work in the Kohlhaasenbruck stables, if necessary with a whip. And when Herse, no sooner had he heard these words, cried out: "Sir, this very day, if possible!" and tossed his cap in the air and assured him he would have a rope made with ten knots to teach him to currycomb! than Kohlhaas sold the house, packed the children in a carriage and dispatched them over the border; called, as night fell, all his remaining servants, seven in number, each and every one trustworthy as gold; armed and mounted them, and set off for Tronkenburg.

With this small band at nightfall three days later, riding down the tollkeeper and the sentry who were standing talking in the gateway, he attacked the castle, and as the little hutments in the castle yard suddenly went crackling up in flames, and Herse raced up the spiral staircase to the castle keep and ambushed the castellan and the steward as they sat at dice in their shirts, Kohlhaas himself plunged into Junker Wenzel's apartments. In just the same way does the Angel of Justice descend from heaven; and the Junker, who was reading to loud laughter to a circle of his young friends the ultimatum the horse dealer had sent him, failed to hear his voice in the yard: sighting him, the blood drained from his face, and he cried out: Brothers, save yourselves! and disappeared. Kohlhaas on entering the room confronted the knight Hans von Tronka, grabbed him by the scruff and hurled him into a corner, where his brains were dashed out against the stone, then, while his comrades were overwhelming and scattering the other knights, who had reached for their weapons, asked where was Wenzel? And getting no help from the insensate men, he kicked open the doors to two chambers that led to further wings of the castle and finding no one at home in the rambling premises, so, swearing, he descended to the yard, to have the exits watched. By now, the fire from the hutments had gripped the castle itself and its side buildings, sending thick smoke heavenward, and while Sternbald with three assiduous grooms was piling up and emptying out everything that was not made fast, between the horses, as booty, from the opened windows of the castle keep to Herse's shout of triumph, the bodies of the castellan and steward were defenestrated, along with those of their wives and children. When the old gouty woman who oversaw the Junker's household threw herself at Kohlhaas's feet, he asked, briefly pausing on the step, where was Wenzel von Tronka? And when she replied with weak, quaking voice, she supposed he might have taken refuge in the chapel, he called to a couple of grooms with torches, had, for want of a key, the door broken down with irons and axes, threw over altars and pews, and still to his fury and consternation, found no trace of the Junker. It so happened that just as Kohlhaas was leaving the chapel, a young servant belonging to the Tronkenburg household was hurrying by to rescue the Junker's warhorses from a stone stable that was threatened by the flames. Kohlhaas, catching sight of his own two in a small adjacent thatched stable asked him: Why not these horses? To which, putting the key in the lock of the stable, the lad replied: That shed was already well alight; at which Kohlhaas violently pulled the key out of the lock, and tossed it over the wall, then forced the boy, hitting him repeatedly with the flat of his blade, to run into the burning shed, and to the grisly laughter of the spectators, made him rescue the horses. When, moments after the shed collapsed, he stood outside with the bridles in his hand, still pale with fear, he found Kohlhaas no longer there; and joining the grooms in the castle yard, he asked the horse breeder who several times turned his back on him, what would he have him do with the animals now?—and Kohlhaas with a terrifying gesture raised his boot so that, if he had struck him, it would certainly have been his death; without giving him an answer he mounted his steed, settled himself in the gateway, and waited, while his band continued their activities, for the silent approach of the new day.

When morning broke, the whole castle was burned down to its foundations, and no one was left within but Kohlhaas and his seven men. He got off his horse, and now by light of day inspected every nook and cranny, and since he was forced to concede, much against his hope, that the enterprise against the castle had failed, with his breast full of pain and bitterness, he sent out Herse with a couple of others to find news as to the direction of the Junker's flight. He had particular suspicions regarding a wealthy establishment situated on the banks of the river Mulde, a convent by the name of Erlabrunn, whose abbess, Antonia von Tronka, was locally known as a devout, charitable, and holy woman; to the unhappy Kohlhaas it seemed all too likely that the Junker, stripped of all his means, might have fled there, where his aunt who had raised him from infancy, was the abbess. Having been apprised of the position, Kohlhaas climbed up the tower of the keep, within which there was left one habitable room, and composed his so-called Kohlhaas Edict, in which he ordered the country to refuse all assistance to the Junker Wenzel von Tronka with whom he was engaged in a just war, rather obliging every inhabitant to hand over said party to him if found, under pain of death and the inevitable incineration of whatever property he might own. This decree he distributed, by means of travelers and visitors, far and wide; yes, he gave his groom Waldmann a copy of it with the specific instruction to put it in the hands of Sister Antonia in Erlabrunn. Hereupon he spoke to some of the Tronkenburg staff who were unhappy with the Junker, and tempted by the prospect of booty, desired to enter into his service; he armed them as infantrymen with crossbows and daggers, and instructed them to sit up behind his mounted grooms; and once he had turned everything his band had brought together to money, and distributed it among them all, he rested for a few hours in the gatehouse, from his dismal business.

Towards noon, Herse returned and confirmed what in his gloomy heart of hearts he had always suspected: namely that the Junker was indeed at Erlabrunn with his old aunt Antonia von Tronka. It appeared he had fled through a door at the back of the castle that led out into the open, and then down a narrow flight of stone steps under a small roof and so gained access to the banks of the Elbe, where he had untied a boat. Herse reported that he had fetched up in a village on the Elbe, to the astonishment of the locals who had assembled because of the fire in Tronkenburg, at around midnight, in a skiff, without oars or rudder, and had traveled on to Erlabrunn in a village cart. Kohlhaas heaved a deep sigh when he heard this, and asked if the horses had been fed. And when he was told that they had, he ordered his band to mount and three hours later they were in Erlabrunn. A storm was rumbling on the horizon as they moved into the convent yard, with lit torches, and Waldmann the groom came out to meet them, reporting that he had delivered the edict as instructed, when he saw the abbess and the chief steward in whispered conversation emerge from the doorway; and while the one, the steward, a small, old, white-haired man darting furious looks at Kohlhaas, was just being girded in his armor, and called with bold voice to the servants who were helping him to pull the storm bell, she, the abbess, pale as a sheet, with a silver image of Our Lord in her hand, descended, and with all her sisters threw herself down before Kohlhaas's horse. While Sternbald and Herse overcame the unarmed steward, taking him back as a prisoner among the horses, Kohlhaas asked her: Where was the Junker Wenzel von Tronka? And she, loosing a large key ring from her belt: In Wittenberg, sir, adding with trembling voice: Go in fear of the Lord and do no wrong!—then Kohlhaas, back in the Hell of unsatisfied vengeance, turned his horse, and was on the point of calling out: Burn everything! when a great bolt of lightning struck the ground beside him. Turning his horse to face the abbess

again, Kohlhaas asked her if she had received his edict? And
when the lady, in feeble, barely audible tones, replied, yes!—
When?—Two hours ago, so god help me, after the Junker,
my cousin, fled!—and Waldmann, to whom Kohlhaas turned
with thunderous brow, stammered his confirmation, claiming that the state of the Mulde, swelled by rain, had delayed
his arrival: then Kohlhaas, collecting himself; a sudden tor-
rential downpour put out the torches, pattering down on the
cobbled yard, allowed the pain to escape his unhappy breast;
doffing his hat to the lady, he turned his horse, set spurs to its
flanks, and with the words: Brothers, follow me, the Junker is
in Wittenberg! he left the convent.

Night falling, he turned into an inn on the highway, where,
because the horses were exhausted, he was forced to rest up
for a day, and fully understanding that with a band of ten
men (because that was their current strength) he was unable to defy a place the size of Wittenberg, he drew up a
second decree, in which, after briefly describing his travails,
he challenged as he put it "every good Christian, for a wage
and other advantages of war to take up his cause against the
Junker von Tronka, the enemy of all Christians." In a further
decree, soon to appear, he called himself "a free man who
knew no lord over him but God Himself"; a misconceived
and deranged arrogation that nevertheless, along with the
color of his money and the prospect of booty, brought him
a following among the crowd that had lost their living with
the conclusion of peace with Poland; so much so in fact that
before long he counted thirty and more heads as he moved
along the right bank of the Elbe, purposing the destruction
of Wittenberg. With his horses and men he pitched camp
under the roof of an old decrepit brick barn in the solitude of

the gloomy forest that then surrounded it, and subsequently having made the discovery through his agent Sternbald, whom he dispatched in disguise into the town with a copy of the decree, that the decree was already well-known, he broke out with his men on the eve of Whitsun, and while the inhabitants were fast asleep in their beds, he torched the town in several places. While his men were plundering the outskirts, he made fast a notice to a pillar of the church to the effect that "he, Kohlhaas, had lit the town, and, if the Junker be not surrendered to me, I will proceed to demolish it," as he put it, "so that there be not two stones upon one another for him to hide behind."

The horror of the inhabitants about this awful crime was indescribable; and the flames that, in what was fortunately a calm summer night, destroyed no more than nineteen houses, admittedly including a church, were not quite put out towards break of day when the old Governor, Otto von Gorgas, sent out a detachment of fifty men to arrest the rabid aggressor. The commander of this detachment, a man by the name of Gerstenberg, comported himself so inadequately that Kohlhaas's force, far from being defeated, acquired a dangerous reputation for military prowess; for once this soldier broke up his men in several groups, with the intention of surrounding and defeating Kohlhaas, the very opposite happened, and Kohlhaas, keeping his band together, counterattacked, assaulted, and defeated him at different points, to the degree that the following evening not one member of the detachment that had had the hopes of the entire province placed in it, survived to oppose him in the field. Kohlhaas, who himself had suffered negligible losses in the fighting, torched the town again the following morning, and his murderous efforts this time were so successful that a number of houses and almost all the outlying barns and granaries went up in flames. At the same time, he made sure to put up the afore-described decree again, audaciously selecting for his purpose the corner of the town hall itself, adding a postscript about the fate of Gerstenberg, the Governor's handpicked commander, who now lay dead. The Governor, infuriated by this proof of defiance, set himself with a few other knights at the head of a column of some hundred and fifty fighters. He gave Wenzel von Tronka, in response to the latter's written request, an armed guard to protect him from violence from the populace, who plainly wanted him gone; and after setting up sentries on the walls and in all the villages round about to protect them from attack, he himself moved out on St. Gervasius's Day, to capture the fire-breathing dragon that was laying waste the land. The horse breeder was clever enough to stay out of his way, and after cannily luring the Governor five miles out of town by marching hither and thither and by various ruses leading him to the mistaken supposition that, oppressed by his greater numbers, he was about to retreat into Brandenburg; he suddenly at nightfall of the third day, turned about and with a forced gallop returned to Wittenberg, where for the third time he torched the town. It was Herse, creeping into the town in disguise, who was responsible for this appalling trick; and the fire this time, driven by a powerful wind from the north, was so destructive and all-consuming that in the space of three hours, forty-two houses, two churches, several cloisters and schools, and the headquarters of the government itself were reduced to smoke and ashes. The Governor who at the beginning of the day had believed his enemy in Brandenburg, hearing the news, found, when he doubled back, the town in uproar over what had happened; the populace had assembled, several thousand strong, outside the house of the Junker bolted and barred with beams, with loud calls for his removal from the town. Two Mayors, Jenkens and Otto were their names, who were present in official garb at the head of the entire magistracy, vainly argued that they should wait for the return of an envoy who had been sent to the President of the Chancellery in Dresden, to request permission to move the Junker there, where he had several reasons for wanting to be. The mob, however, armed with pikes and cudgels, were not interested in his words, and were getting close to storming the house, manhandling some of the aldermen who were advocating dire measures against them, and leveling it, when the Governor, Otto von Gorgas, at the head of his cavalry, appeared in the town. This worthy gentleman, used to striking awe and obedience in the people through his mere presence, had succeeded just outside town, and as a sort of compensation for his failed larger objective, in capturing three individuals from the band of the murderous arsonist; and since, as the villains were being loaded with chains in full view of the crowd, he assured the magistrate in a clever speech that the next man to arrive in chains would be Kohlhaas himself, as he was now on his tail, so he was able, with these various calming measures, to disarm the panic of the crowd, and allay their concerns as to the presence of the Junker, at least until the return of the envoy from Dresden. In the company of some of his horsemen, he now dismounted, and removing palisades and posts, he made his way into the house, where he found the Junker, who was tumbling from one spell of unconsciousness to the next, in the hands of a couple of doctors, seeking to restore him to life with the help of various essences and stimulants; and since von Gorgas felt this was not the right moment for a conversation, because of the riot that had been provoked, he contented himself with saying, with a look of quiet contempt, that he should get dressed, and for his own safety, follow him to the prison. When the Junker had been clad in a tunic, and a helmet slapped on his head, and he appeared on the street, half-unlaced because of his difficulty breathing, leaning on the arm of the Governor and of his brother-in-law, Count von Gerschau, the most blasphemous and bloodcurdling curses were sent heavenward. The crowd, with difficulty held back by the armed guards, called him a leach, a miserable pestilence and tormentor, a curse upon Wittenberg, and the ruin of Saxony; and after a miserable transit through the ruined town, in the course of which he several times lost his helmet without apparently missing it, each time having it picked up and returned to him by a rider, they finally reached the prison, where he disappeared up a tower, under the protection of an armed guard. But now the return of the envoy with the decision of the Elector plunged the town into fresh anxiety. For the provincial government, to which the citizenry of Dresden had made an urgent appeal, would not hear of accommodating the Junker in the capital before the apprehension of the arsonist and murderer; rather it instructed the Governor to keep him safe wherever he was—and he had to be somewhere—to protect him with all the force he had at his disposal, and to the relief of the good town of Wittenberg, it reported that an army of five hundred men, under the command of Prince Friedrich of Meissen, was advancing, to shield it from further depredations of this same. The Governor well understood that no resolution of this sort was capable of allaying the fears of the crowd, for not only had the horse breeder fought several successful skirmishes outside the town already, but the strength of his numbers was now the subject of unpleasant rumor; the war that he had fought, with disguised agents, with pitch and straw and sulfur, unexampled and terrible as it was, was enough to laugh to scorn far greater protection than that offered now by the Prince of Meissen. The Governor on cursory reflection decided to suppress all news of the government's decision. He merely posted in the four corners of the town a letter in which the Prince of Meissen announced his imminent arrival; a covered wagon that left the yard of the castle keep at daybreak escorted by four heavily armed horsemen went out on the Leipzig road, with the horsemen giving it to be understood that they were headed for Pleissenburg; and since the mob was now relieved about the troublesome Junker, whose existence had brought fire and sword down upon them, some three hundred men now volunteered to join the forces of the Prince of Meissen. Kohlhaas in the meantime, because of the odd place he occupied in the world, now found himself at the head of some hundred and nine men; and since he had come upon another store of weapons in Jassen, and was now able to outfit and equip his men fully, informed of the twin forces that were coming his way, he took the decision to meet this twofold threat head on, and with the speed of the wind, before their joined forces were able to destroy him. Accordingly, the very next day he attacked the Prince of Meissen in a night raid at Mühlberg; in the course of the battle, to his great grief, he lost Herse, who collapsed at his side in the course of an early exchange of fire; but embittered by the loss, in a three hour battle he had done so much damage to the Prince's forces, unable to rally or regroup, that at daybreak, the latter, gravely wounded and with his troops routed, was forced to march back to Dresden.

Further emboldened by this success, even before news of it got out, Kohlhaas now turned his attention back to the Governor, and fell upon him in the village of Damerow in broad daylight and open country, and, admittedly incurring murderous losses, inflicted similar damage upon this foe by nightfall. Yes, he would have gone on to attack the Governor, who lay in the churchyard at Damerow with the remnants of his force, a second time had not the latter been informed by spies of the defeat suffered at Mühlberg by the Prince of Meissen, and so thought it prudent, in similar fashion, to retire to Wittenberg and wait for another occasion. Five days after scattering both his enemies, Kohlhaas was outside Leipzig, and set it on fire in three different places.

In the edict he gave out on this occasion, he referred to himself as "a vice-regent of the Archangel Michael, come to punish with fire and sword all those who took the side of the Junker, the wickedness in which this whole world has sunk." So saying, he called on the people from the castle at Lützen, which he had taken and where he had now installed himself, to join him towards building a better organization of the world; and this edict he megalomaniacally signed, "issued from the seat of our provisional world government, the fortress at Lützen." The luck of the Leipzigers meant that, because of a persistent rain from heaven, the fire was unable to spread, and, with the speed of the fire-extinguishing measures, only a few shops situated around Pleissenburg went up in flames. At the same time, though, the shock of the city as to the presence of the murderous arsonist at their gates and his attachment to the belief that the Junker was in their city, was inexpressible. And since a detachment of 180 cavalry that had been sent against him returned scattered and defeated, so the authorities, unwilling to risk the wealth of their city, had no option but to lock all the gates, and have those that lived outwith watched day and night. Vainly did the town government have proclamations put up in the outlying villages assuring them that the Junker was not present in Pleissenburg; the horse breeder, in proclamations of his own, insisted that he was, and explained that even if he weren't, he, Kohlhaas, still meant to proceed as though he were, until such time as he was told his actual whereabouts. The Elector, informed by an envoy of the dire situation of the city of Leipzig, said that he had already gathered an army of two thousand men, and was putting himself at their head, to go and catch Kohlhaas. He gave Otto von Gorgas a severe rebuke for his doubtful and facile scheme to get the arsonist away from the vicinity of Wittenberg; and no one can describe the confusion of the whole of Saxony and in particular the villages outside Leipzig when it was learned—the source is not known—that a declaration had been put up to Kohlhaas, claiming: "The Junker Wenzel is with his cousins Hinz and Kunz, in Dresden."

These were the circumstances when Doctor Martin Luther took it upon himself, with soothing language, and using the power of his standing in the world, to return Kohlhaas to the ordinary bounds of human society, and addressing himself to a strand of decency in the arsonist's heart, he published the following letter to him, which he had posted in towns and villages throughout the Electorate:

> Kohlhaas, you claim to be on a mission, you have taken up the sword of justice, you are the mad slave to an irrational passion, a vessel of injustice from head to toe, what are you arrogating to yourself? Because the Sovereign whose subject you are has refused you justice, justice in a squabble over something worth nothing, you arise,

you desperado, with fire and sword, and like a desert wolf break into the peaceful community that he protects. You, who misleads people with your claim full of untruths and wickedness: do you think, sinner that you are, that when the day comes, your tactics will confuse God, who sees into every wrinkle of every heart? How can you claim to have been denied your rights, you, whose violent heart, tickled by crude vengeance, has completely given up seeking them, once your first facile attempts failed? Is the authority you respect a line of placemen and creatures, who cause a document to disappear, or contrive to deny an inevitable judgment? Must I tell you, godforsaken man, that the authorities know nothing of this matter—what? That the Sovereign you are rebelling against does not so much as know your name, so that when you one day appear before the Almighty's throne and bring your complaint against him, he, with unruffled features, will say: Lord, I have done this man no wrong, his very existence is unknown to my soul. Know that the sword you brandish is the sword of rapine and murder, you are a rebel and not a righteous warrior before the Lord, and your earthly destination is none but the wheel and the gallows, and in the hereafter the damnation that befalls the criminal and those who are without God.

Wittenberg, etc.   *Martin Luther*

In the fortress at Lützen, Kohlhaas was just in his unhappy soul revolving a fresh plan to consign Leipzig to the ashes— for he gave no credence to the notice put up in the villages that Junker Wenzel was in Dresden, because it had no signature appended to it, and certainly not that of the magistrate, as he had demanded—when Sternbald and Waldmann spotted the poster that to their dismay had been put up overnight in the entryway to the castle. Vainly they continued to hope over several days that Kohlhaas, whom they were unwilling to approach in the matter, would see it himself; grim and introverted, he did step out in the evening sometimes, but just to give his curt orders, and saw nothing: so that one morning, when he ordered the hanging of a couple of fellows who had been caught plundering in the area against his wishes, they resolved to draw his attention to it. He was just on his way back from the execution place, the people shyly retreating from him on either side, in the costume he had been affecting since his latest edict: a long broadsword on a red morocco cushion with golden tassels borne along in front of him, and twelve squires bearing torches following after: just then the two men, swords tucked under their arms to attract his attention, turned at the pillar where the bill had been posted. When Kohlhaas passed under the archway, his hands clasped behind his back, lost in thought, he opened his eyes and gave a start; and since the squires respectfully ducked out of the way, so, looking at them confusedly, he took a few rapid strides up to the pillar. Who will describe what went on inside him when he saw that paper that accused him of injustice: and signed by the dearest and most respect-worthy name he knew, that of Martin Luther! A dark blush mantled his countenance, he took off his helmet and read what was in front of him twice through; then, looking uncertain, he turned back into the midst of his fellows, as though to speak to them, though he said nothing; pulled the paper off the wall, read it a third time, and called out: Waldmann, I want my horse saddled! and: Sternbald, follow me into the castle! and he disappeared. It needed no more than those few words to suddenly reveal him to himself in his full abomination. He slipped into the clothes of a Thuringian tenant farmer; told Sternbald that some business of passing importance compelled him to travel to Wittenberg; entrusted him, in the presence of several of his lieutenants, with the command of the remaining troop at Lützen; and with the assurance that he would be back in three days, and there was no reason to expect any attack before then, he left for Wittenberg.

Under an alias he put up at an inn, where, no sooner had it got dark, than swathed in a cloak, and with a pair of pistols he had acquired in Tronkenburg, he stepped into Luther's room. Luther seated at his desk with books and papers, seeing the unfamiliar, rather fearsome-looking fellow open the door and bolt it after him, asked who he was and what he wanted, and no sooner had the visitor, holding his hat reverently in his hand with the shy anticipation of the terror he would cause, replied that he was Michael Kohlhaas, the horse breeder, than Luther cried out: Get away from me! And rising from his desk to a bell added: Your breath is pestilence and your proximity destruction! Kohlhaas, drawing his pistol but otherwise not moving, said: Respected sir, this pistol, if you touch the bell, will leave me lifeless at your feet! Sit down and hear me out. You are no safer in the company of the angels whose psalms you record than you are with me. Sitting down, Luther asked: What do you want? Kohlhaas replied: Revise your view of me as an unjust man! You wrote in your pronouncement that the authorities know nothing of my case: well, get me free passage and I will go to Dresden and present it.

"Wicked and appalling man!" exclaimed Luther, simultaneously confused and a little calmed by his words: "Who gave you the right to ambush the Junker von Tronka in the pursuit of your self-appointed justice, and not finding him at home in his castle, to proceed to lay fire and sword to the whole community that protects him?" Kohlhaas replied: Sir, henceforth, no one! Some news I had from Dresden led me astray. The war I am waging against the bulk of mankind is sinful, were it not that I am, as you assure me, cast out from it. Cast out! exclaimed Luther, looking at him. What madness has seized you? Who cast you out of the common state in which you resided? Yes, in the whole history of states, where is there an instance of anyone, whoever he might be, being cast out from it?

Outcast, replied Kohlhaas, clenching his fist, is my word for a man who receives no protection from the law. I need such protection for the peaceful exercise of my profession; yes, that is the sole reason why, together with the fruits of my work, I took refuge in a community. And whosoever would deny me such classes me with the savages of the wild; he gives me, and how can you argue with this, the cudgel with which I protect myself into my hand.

Who denied you the protection of the law? exclaimed Luther. Did I not write that the suit you would bring before the Sovereign is unknown to him? If his ministers conceal things from him, or otherwise, all unbeknown to him, mock his sanctified name; who but God is permitted to call him to account for his choice of ministers, and what gives you the authority, a godforsaken and appalling man, to judge him for it?

Very well, said Kohlhaas, if the Sovereign doesn't cast me out, then I will return to the community he protects. I repeat, secure free passage for me to Dresden, and I'll disband the army I've assembled at the fortress of Lützen, and present the charge that was refused once before, this time at the tribunal of the province.

Luther, with a grim expression, swept the papers off his desk and said nothing. The stubborn attitude this strange man took to the state irked him; and thinking now about the ultimatum that Kohlhaas had drawn up in Kohlhaasenbrück and served to the Junker, he inquired: What did he look to the tribunal at Dresden for? Kohlhaas replied: Punishment for the Junker in accordance with the law; restoration of my horses in their original state; and some recompense for the violence done to us, both for myself and my squire Herse who fell at the battle at Mühlberg.

Luther cried out: Compensation! But you borrowed sums running into thousands from Jews and Christians, for the execution of your wild revenge. Will you be putting those moneys on your bill as well?

Heaven forfend! replied Kohlhaas. I am not asking for the return of my house and lands and comforts, nor the expense of my wife's funeral. Herse's old dam will come out with a calculation of the expenses of healing him, and an itemization of his sufferings in Tronkenburg; and as for the loss I incurred through the lost sale of my two horses, let the government have an actuary assess that.

Luther exclaimed: Mad, baffling and appalling man! And looked at him. After your sword has exacted the bloodiest imaginable retribution on the Junker, what drives you still to look for a judgment against him, whose sharpness when it falls, will be of such trifling weight?

A tear coursing down his cheek, Kohlhaas replied: Sir! It cost me my wife; it is Kohlhaas's wish to prove to the world that she did not perish in an unjust cause. Do as I say in this matter, and let the court speak; in everything else, I will abide by whatever you tell me.

Luther remarked: Listen now, what you ask, if the course

of events was as described, is just; and had you not proceeded impudently to exact your revenge, refusing to await
the Sovereign's decision, then I don't doubt but that your
claim, point by point, would be agreed. But, all things consid-
ered, wouldn't you have done better to forgive the Junker, for
the sake of our Savior, take the horses in hand, thin and exhausted as they were, mounted up, and ridden them home to
your stables in Kohlhaasenbrück to feed them back to health
and condition?

Kohlhaas replied: You may be right, as he stepped up to
the window, maybe, maybe not. If I'd known that I'd have
to restore them with the heart's blood of my dearly loved
wife, then maybe I would have done as you say, sir, and not
begrudged them a bushel of oats! But because they have now
cost me so much, it seems to me, the thing has its own mo-
mentum: now, let judgment come, and the Junker feed my
horses.

Luther said, attending to his papers once more, and re-
flecting variously: He would agree to speak to the Elector on
his behalf. Till that time, he suggested staying quietly in the
fortress at Lützen; if the Elector gave him free passage, then
he would be apprised of it by public bill.

Now, he went on, as Kohlhaas stooped to kiss his hand:
whether the Elector will be lenient with you, I do not know:
because I hear he has assembled an army of his own, and will
march on the fortress at Lützen and arrest you: well, as I say,
it won't be for want of trying on my behalf. And so saying, he
got up and made to let him leave. Kohlhaas said that the mere
fact of his advocacy was enough to settle him: whereupon
Luther raised his hand in farewell, but the other suddenly
dropped to one knee before him, and said he had one further
desire of him. He was in the habit of attending Mass, and at

Whitsun he had missed church on account of his warring; would he have the kindness, without further ado, to hear him make his confession, and in return do him the kindness of his Holy absolution? Luther thought briefly, looked at him hard, and said: Yes, Kohlhaas, I will. But remember, the Lord, of whose body you desire to partake, forgave His enemies.

Are you willing, he went on, as the other looked at him guiltily, likewise to forgive the Junker who has wronged you: to go to Tronkenburg, mount up on your mares, and ride them home to Kohlhaasenbrück to health and fitness?

Reverend sir, said a blushing Kohlhaas, clasping his hand—Well?—The Lord did not forgive all His enemies. I will forgive the Elector, the two gentlemen the castellan and the steward, the other two gentlemen Hinz and Kunz, and whoever else may have offended me in this affair: but if possible, make the Junker feed my horses back to health."

On hearing these words, Luther, with a deprecating look, turned his back on the visitor and rang the bell. While the servant thus summoned came in with a candle to the ante-room, Kohlhaas got guiltily to his feet, wiping a tear from his eye; as the servant was unable to enter, because the door had been bolted, and Luther sat down again at his manuscripts, Kohlhaas admitted the man himself. Luther, with a curt look at the visitor, said to the servant: Light him out! Whereupon the servant, a little surprised by the presence of a stranger, took down the house key from the wall, and waiting for the man to follow him, stood in the doorway.

Twisting his hat in his hands, Kohlhaas said: Is there no way, most respected sir, that I can receive the benediction I asked of you? Luther replied curtly: From your Savior, no; from the Sovereign—as I told you, I will try. And with that he gestured to the servant to carry out his instruction without further delay. With a pained expression, Kohlhaas crossed his hands on his chest, followed the servant who lit him the way down the stairs, and disappeared.

The following morning, Luther drew up a letter to the Elector of Saxony, in which, after bitter aspersions at the presence at court of the Tronkas, Hinz and Kunz, the Chamberlain and cupbearer, who as was widely known, had suppressed the charge, with the frankness that was characteristic of him he told the Sovereign that in such vexatious circumstances there was no option but to accept the horse dealer's suggestion and give him an amnesty and allow his case to go forward. Public opinion, he wrote, was in a most threatening way on the man's side, such that even in the thrice burned-down Wittenberg they were unanimous in his support; and since, if his request were turned down, he would inevitably, with hateful accusations, make it public knowledge, and the people could easily be misled to the degree that the state would be powerless to do anything against him. He concluded by saying that in this unusual case the embargo on entering into negotiations with a citizen who had taken up arms against the state would have to be set aside; that the said individual, by virtue of the ill-treatment he had received, had in a sense, been made to quit the polity; and in a word, that to escape from this predicament, it were better to view him as a foreign invader—which, as a non-Saxon, in a sense he was—than as the leader of a rebellion against the crown.

The Elector received this letter just as Prince Christian von Meissen, supreme commander-in-chief of the Emperor, and the uncle of that Prince Friedrich von Meissen lately defeated at Mühlberg and still gravely ill with his wounds; the Lord Chancellor, Count Wrede; Count Kallheim, President of the

Chancellery; and the courtiers Hinz and Kunz von Tronka, one a Chamberlain and the other the cupbearer, boyhood friends and confidants of their master, were all assembled in the castle. The Chamberlain—Kunz—who in his capacity as Private Secretary was responsible for the Elector's diplomatic correspondence, and had the right to use his name and seal, spoke first, and after explaining at length that he would never have wantonly turned down the complaint that the horse breeder had made against his cousin the Junker, had he not, misled by false information, taken it to be a completely baseless and futile bit of peevishness, eventually got around to things as they presently stood. He observed that neither divine nor human law supported the horse breeder—on account of a legal error—in such monstrous vengeance as he had permitted himself; he described the sheen of glory that would cover his infamous head through negotiating with the ruler as a legitimate foe; and the humiliation that, *eo ipso*, would redound to the sacred person of the Elector struck him as so unbearable, that in his garrulousness and zeal he thought it preferable to bite the bullet and fulfill the demands of the deranged rebel, and have the Junker, his cousin, led away to Kohlhaasenbrück to feed the horses, than to accept the suggestion put forward by Doctor Luther. The Lord Chancellor, Count Wrede, half-turning towards him, voiced regret that such sensitivity as he now displayed for the good name of the ruler had not actuated him any sooner. He told the Elector of his doubts concerning the use of state power to put into effect an evidently unlawful measure; observed, with a speaking look at the popularity the horse dealer was finding throughout the country, that the whole long string of his crimes was threatening to go on into endlessness; and argued that only an act of simple righteousness, as here by immediately and wholly taking back the wrongful treatment incurred, was capable of breaking it off and extricating the government in reasonable shape from the whole unpleasant situation. Prince von Meissen, asked by the ruler for his views, observed, turning respectfully in the direction of the Lord Chancellor: The habits of thought he displayed filled him with the greatest respect; however, in helping Kohlhaas to obtain justice, he was failing to consider that he was curtailing the justified expectations of Wittenberg and Leipzig and the whole abused territory of compensation, or, at the very least, merited punishment. The good order of the state, with respect to this individual, was so grievously upset that it would hardly be possible to restore it with recourse to law. This being so, he joined the Chamberlain in advocating the use of the traditional means in such cases: to assemble an army of sufficient strength, and to either arrest or crush the horse trader at Lützen, as the case might be. The Chamberlain, bringing chairs for the Prince and the Elector, and pushing them into the room, said he was pleased that a man of his uprightness and insight agreed with him as to the best way of solving this vexatious matter. The Prince, holding the back of the chair and not sitting in it, looked at him and assured him: That he had no cause to feel pleased, as the measure would involve a summons for his arrest, and a case against him in court for misuse of the Sovereign's name and title. For if a veil had to be lowered before the throne of justice, and over a series of brazen crimes that reached to the distant horizon, that was not the case with the initial wrong; and it was only the bringing against Kunz of a capital charge that would allow the state to proceed to the crushing of the horse breeder, whose cause was, as agreed, entirely just, and the sword in whose hand had been put there by actors purporting to represent the state. The Elector whom Kunz now looked at apprehensively, turned, his entire face flushing, and crossed the chamber to the window. Following a protracted silence on all quarters, Count Kallheim said this did nothing to extract them from the vicious circle in which they found themselves. Why, it was every bit as justified to bring charges against the Prince's nephew, Friedrich, because he too, in the sweeping emergency action he had taken against Kohlhaas, had exceeded the terms of his remit; if one asked for the numerous individuals who had been prompted by the perplexity of the situation to take action, he would certainly be among those named, and would have to be charged by the Sovereign for the sorry events at Mühlberg. As the Elector with inscrutable mien returned to the table, the cupbearer, Hinz von Tronka, now took the floor, and remarked that he didn't understand how the correct course of action could escape men of such wisdom as those assembled here. It was his understanding that the horse breeder had promised to disband the force with which he had laid waste the country in exchange for the promise of a safe conduct to Dresden and the reopening of the investigation into his case. This was not at all the same thing as an amnesty for his vicious campaign of vengeance; these were two distinct legal terms which both Doctor Luther and the Council seemed to be confounding. If, he resumed, touching his finger to the side of his nose, the tribunal at Dresden decides one way over the horses, that in no way precludes the arrest of Kohlhaas for his murderous campaign of arson and rampage: a very politic decision that combines the advantages of both opposing views, and is certain of the applause of the world and posterity.

Seeing both the Prince and the Chancellor respond to this argument with mere looks at Hinz, the meeting seemed to be at an end, and the Elector said that before the next session of the Council he would consider the various courses of action that had been presented to him.

It seemed that the Prince's idea of bringing preliminary charges against Kunz had robbed the rather softhearted Elector of the desire to conduct the campaign against Kohlhaas for which otherwise everything had been made ready. He kept back his Chancellor, Count Wrede, whose views seemed most to the point; and when Wrede proceeded to show the ruler documents from which it appeared that the strength of the horse breeder had now grown to four hundred armed men; yes, and considering the general dissatisfaction over the irregularities of the Chamberlain that was abroad in the land, could well rapidly double and treble in number; then the Elector decided, without further ado, to accept the suggestion of Doctor Luther. He put Count Wrede in charge of the entire Kohlhaas affair, and not many days later, a notice appeared the gist of which ran as follows:

"His Royal Highness the Elector of Saxony, taking especial cognizance of a letter from Doctor Martin Luther, hereby extends to Michael Kohlhaas, horse breeder and subject of Brandenburg, upon condition that he disarms within three days of sight of this posting, a safe conduct to Dresden, for a reopening of his legal affair; a proviso being that if, as seems unlikely, his suit concerning the treatment of his horses is rejected by the court, he will be subject to the full severity of the law for the high-handedness of his personal quest for justice; in the contrary case, however, mercy will be extended to both the man and his followers, and a complete amnesty will be granted for any acts of violence and destruction carried out in Saxony."

No sooner had Kohlhaas received a copy—from Doctor

Luther—of this bill posted in all public squares of the land, than, however hedged about with conditionality of the language, he immediately disbanded his force, with presents, expressions of thanks and earnest warnings. He deposited all he had in terms of money, arms, and equipment with the court at Lützen, as belonging to the Crown; and once he had dispatched Waldmann with letters regarding the possible repurchase of his farm, to his neighbor in Kohlhaasenbrück, and Sternbald to Schwerin, to collect his children, with whom he wished to be reunited, he left the fortress at Lützen, and made his way, incognito, with what remained of his small fortune, which he carried with him in the form of papers, to Dresden.

Day was just breaking, and the whole city was still asleep when he knocked on the door of a small property that, thanks to the punctiliousness of his neighbor, remained to him in Pirna just outside Dresden, and he said to Thomas, the old porter who ran the establishment for him, and now with bewilderment and apprehension admitted him, that he was to report to the Prince of Meissen in the palace that he, Kohlhaas the horse breeder, had rendered himself. The Prince of Meissen, who thought it worth his while to get an accurate picture of where one stood in relation to this individual, found, when with a retinue of knights and squires he rode round there, that there was already an innumerable mass of people foregathered in the streets surrounding Kohlhaas's apartment. The news of the arrival of the destroying angel who pursued the oppressors of the people with fire and sword had caused all Dresden, city and surroundings, to turn out; those within were forced to bolt the doors against the curious crowd of onlookers, and the little ones scampered up the windows to catch a glimpse of the murderous arsonist at breakfast. As soon as the Prince, his attendants clearing the way for him, had got inside the house, and had stepped into Kohlhaas's room, he asked the man standing there by a table, half-dressed: Was he indeed Kohlhaas the horse breeder? To which Kohlhaas, taking from his belt a wallet that contained various papers identifying him, and respectfully handing them to him, replied in the affirmative, adding that following the required disbanding of his troop, he was taking advantage of the Sovereign's offer of a safe conduct, and was come to Dresden to pursue the case against the Junker Wenzel von Tronka about his horses. The Prince, eyeing the man from head to foot, went through the papers in the wallet; heard an explanation concerning the certificate issued by the court at Lützen he came upon, as to the transfer of certain valuables to the Elector's exchequer; and after various further questions regarding the character of the man before him, his children, his fortune, and the manner of life he intended to pursue in future, established in each particular that there was no cause for the least concern, returned the documents to him and remarked that there was nothing there to hinder his pursuit of the case, and that he should seek out the Lord Chancellor, Count Wrede, in person to take the next steps. And for the time being, observed the Prince, walking up to the window and gazing in some astonishment at the mass of humanity outside, you should ask for a guard for the first few days to protect the house, and your person when you step out.

Kohlhaas looked down in dismay and said nothing. "No matter," said the Prince, turning away from the window. "You'll have to see for yourself what happens," and so saying, he turned to the door, to leave the house. Kohlhaas, having thought a moment, said: Sir, as you please! Just give me your word that the guard will be withdrawn the moment I ask. Then I'll have nothing against such a measure. The Prince replied that that surely went without saying, and after he'd presented and left behind three armed men, telling them that the man in the house was free to come and go as he pleased, they were merely to escort him to his protection, he waved airily in the direction of the horse breeder, and left.

Towards noon, under escort from his three armed men, and followed by a great mob of people who, having been warned by the police, did nothing to harm him, he went to see Count Wrede. The Lord Chancellor, greeting him with cordiality in his anteroom, talked to him for all of two hours, and having asked for an account of the whole history from beginning to end, gave him the name of a celebrated and highly accredited lawyer in the city, who would frame and submit his charge. Without any more ado, Kohlhaas made for the man's apartments, and after the composition of the complaint, like its rejected predecessor, requiring the punishment of the Junker in accordance with the law, the restoration of the horses to their prior condition, and the payment of compensation for his own losses, as well as those suffered by his servant Herse, fallen at Mühlberg, payable to his old mother, he returned, once more with the accompaniment of the still gawping crowd, to his house, resolved not to leave it again unless for essential business.

In the meantime, the Junker had been released from his protective custody in Wittenberg, and once he had recovered from a dangerous inflammation of the foot, found himself peremptorily summoned by the court to Dresden to answer the case brought against him by the horse breeder Kohlhaas for wrongful taking of his horses and the ruination of same. His Tronka cousins, the Chamberlain and cupbearer, in whose house he put up, welcomed him with the profoundest bitterness and contempt; they called him a miserable wretch who had brought nothing but shame and scandal to the entire family, predicted that he was certain to lose his case, and told him to make arrangements for the procuring of the horses to the fattening up of which he would shortly, to the derision of the world, find himself sentenced. In a feeble, shaking voice the Junker declared himself to be the most pitiful wretch in the world. He swore that of the whole accursed trick that had plunged him into misery he knew next to nothing, that his castellan and steward were responsible for all of it, without his knowledge or approval they had set the horses to work in the harvest and by the excessive strain of the work, part of it on fields that were their own property, ruined them. So saying, he sat down, and begged them not to plunge him wantonly back into the calamity from which he had only just emerged by insulting and offending him. The next day Messrs. Hinz and Kunz, who owned estates not far from the destroyed Tronkenburg, wrote at the request of the Junker their cousin, because there really was no alternative, to their own stewards and tenant farmers for news of the horses that had been lost on that unhappy day and had subsequently disappeared. But all they were able to glean, in view of the demolition of house and estate, and the massacre of almost all the inhabitants, was that a stable boy, driven to it by blows with the flat of the arsonist's sword, had rescued the horses from the burning stable where they were, but the fellow, in answer to his question what he should do with them, and where he should take them, had received a kick from the violent maniac and nothing more. The Junker's ancient gout-ridden housekeeper who had fled to Meissen assured him, in answer to his written inquiry, that, following that appalling night, the stable boy, with the horses, had taken off for Brandenburg; but all efforts there were futile, and the story seemed to be founded on a misapprehension, because the Junker had no squire who hailed from Brandenburg, or even from that general direction. Some men from Dresden who had been in Wilsdruf a matter of days after the burning of Tronkenburg, declared that at that time a young fellow had arrived leading two horses, and had left them in a wretched state and unable to go on, in the cow stall of a shepherd, who had agreed to look after them. For various reasons, it seemed highly plausible that these were indeed the horses in question; but the Wilsdruf shepherd, had, as certain local people claimed, traded them on to some other party, it was not known who; then there was a third report, whose origin remained unknown, according to which the horses were already in Abraham's bosom, and were buried in the knackery at Wilsdruf.

Messrs. Hinz and Kunz, to whom such a turn of events, for understandable reasons, was the most welcome, because it meant that, with the Junker no longer possessing any stables of his own, they were now absolved from the duty of housing the horses in their own, and feeding them up, nevertheless desired, for the sake of complete certainty, to have this fact confirmed. Accordingly Wenzel von Tronka, as local property owner and householder, sent a letter to the courts at Wilsdruf, in which he kindly asked these same, following a detailed description of the two horses, which, he said, had been entrusted to him, and from whom he had been separated by an accident, to establish their present whereabouts, and ask the owner, whoever he might be, to deliver them, against payment of all costs, to the stables of Herr Kunz of Dresden. Whereupon, only a few days later, the man who had bought them from the Wilsdruf shepherd, appeared, and led them, made fast to the back of his cart, tottering and emaciated, to the city's marketplace; the bane of it, to Herr Wenzel and still more to the honest Kohlhaas, was that he was the knacker from Döbbeln.

No sooner had Wenzel von Tronka, in the presence of his Chamberlain cousin, heard a rumor that a man had arrived in the city with two black mares that had survived the fire at Tronkenburg, than the two of them, with a few hastily assembled squires betook themselves to the castle square, where, should they indeed prove to be the Kohlhaas horses, he was to take receipt of them, and against expenses lead them home. How crestfallen then were the two knights when they saw clumped around the two-wheeler to which the horses had been secured, a throng of curious onlookers growing by the minute; calling out to one another with howls of laughter, that the horses that threatened to bring down the state were already in the hands of the knacker! The Junker walked around the cart and looked at the wretched beasts that seemed to be on the point of expiring, and said sheepishly: These were not the horses he had taken from Kohlhaas; but Kunz the Chamberlain, casting at him a look of such speechless fury that had it been of iron it would have smashed him to pieces, brushed back his coat, showing off his medals and chain, stepped up to the knacker, and asked him: Were these the horses that the Wilsdruf shepherd had acquired, and that the Junker Wenzel von Tronka had asked for at the local courts? The knacker, who was carrying a bucket to water the portly nag that drew his cart, asked: "Them black ones?" He brushed the bit from his nag's muzzle after setting down the bucket and said: "The horses that were made fast to the cart had been sold him by the pigman in Hainichen. Where he got them from, if it was the shepherd in Wilsdruf he had no way of knowing." The Wilsdruf court messenger, he went on, picking up the bucket, and jamming it between the axle and his knee, "he said he was to bring them to Dresden to the house of the Tronkas, but the Junker he was told to see, his name were Kunz." And with these words, he tipped the rest of the water from the bucket out over the cobbles. The Chamberlain, ringed by the mocking crowd, unable to induce the fellow to look at him as he mechanically went at his tasks, said that he was the Chamberlain Kunz von Tronka, and the horses he was to take receipt of belonged to his cousin, who was the Junker; and a fellow who escaped from Tronkenburg when it burned down had gone to the shepherd at Wilsdruf with two horses that had originally been the property of the horse breeder Kohlhaas. He asked the fellow who stood there feet apart, tugging at his hose, whether he hadn't happened to hear about any of this? And whether the pigman at Hainichen couldn't possibly have bought them from the Wilsdruf shepherd, perhaps via a third party?

The knacker, having stood next to his cart and urinated, said, "He had been told to go to Dresden with the horses and take them to the Tronka house and collect some money for them. He didn't have the first idea what he was talking about; and whether they had been owned previously by Peter or Paul or the shepherd at Wilsdruf before the Hainichen pigman got them, it made no difference to him so long as they weren't stolen." And with that, his whip tucked across his shoulders, he headed for a hostelry on the square, with the intention of breaking his fast, as he was hungry. The Chamberlain who had no earthly idea what to make of horses the pigman in Hainichen had sold to the knacker in Döbbeln, and if they weren't actually the ones the devil rode through Saxony, called upon the Junker to intervene; but when he replied with trembling, bloodless lips: It couldn't hurt to buy the horses in any case, be they Kohlhaas's or not; so the Chamberlain, cursing his birth, buttoning up his coat, and wholly at a loss what to do or not to do, stepped back out of the heap of rabble. He called out to one Wenk, a knightly acquaintance of his, who was riding by on the other side of the road, and grimly resolved not to leave the square under the mocking eyes of the crowd that was stifling its laughter, seemingly only waiting for his departure to explode, he asked him to go to the Lord Chancellor, Count Wrede, and through his agency get Kohlhaas to inspect the horses. It so happened that Kohlhaas was present in the Lord Chancellor's rooms, having been summoned there by an usher for various explanations regarding his deposition in Lützen that were required of him, when the knight, with the intention described above, walked into the room; and while the Lord Chancellor got up from his chair with a testy expression, and asked the horse breeder (who was of course not known to the entrant) to stand to one side for a moment with the papers he was holding, while the knight described to him the embarrassment in which the two von Tronkas found themselves. Following the inadequate representations of the courts at Wilsdruf, the knacker from Döbbeln had appeared with horses whose condition was so pitiable that the Junker Wenzel von Tronka was on the point of taking them for those of Kohlhaas; just to exclude all possibility of error, a visual inspection by Kohlhaas was thought to be necessary prior to an eventual purchase and attempted resurrection of the beasts in the knights' stables. "Would you be so good," Wenk concluded, "as to have the horse breeder picked up by the guards at his house, and brought to the market, where the horses are currently to be found." The Lord

Chancellor, taking his spectacles off his nose, said that Wenk was doubly mistaken; firstly, in believing that there was no other way of confirming the identity of the horses than by having Kohlhaas inspect them and secondly, in taking the view that he, the Lord Chancellor, was authorized to have Kohlhaas taken by armed guard to any place of the Junker's choosing. So saying, he introduced him to the horse breeder, who was standing next to him, and sitting down and donning his spectacles again, suggested he apply to him directly.

Kohlhaas, giving by his expression no hint at what might be going on within him, said he was willing to follow him to the market to inspect the horses the knacker had brought into town. While Wenk turned awkwardly in his direction, he walked up to the Lord Chancellor's table once more, and after informing him of several details with papers from his wallet concerning the deposition in Lützen, bade him goodbye; Wenk, flushed crimson, did likewise; and the two men, escorted by three of the Prince of Meissen's lansquenets, walked with a flood of onlookers towards the castle square. The Chamberlain, Herr Kunz, who had fought off the appeals of several of his friends and maintained his place among the populace, opposite the knacker of Döbbeln, straightaway, when Wenk and the horse breeder appeared on the scene, walked up to the latter and asked him, while keeping his sword tucked under his arm as a sign of respect: Were the horses that were standing behind the cart his horses? The horse breeder, modestly touching his hat to the gentleman asking the question, because he didn't know him, without making reply went up to the knacker's cart, followed by all the knights; and glancing up from a distance of ten or twelve steps at the beasts, standing there on trembling legs, their heads lowered, not eating the hay the knacker had thrown down before them: Yes, sir! He turned to the Chamberlain, the knacker is absolutely right, the horses he has tethered to his cart are my horses. And with that, he looked round the ring of gentlemen, touched his hat a second time, and, accompanied by his escort, left the square. At his words, the Chamberlain strode swiftly to the knacker, so that the plumes on his helmet shook, and tossed him a purse of money; and while the knacker, purse in hand, scraped the hair out of his face with a lead comb, and eying the money, he ordered a squire to untie the horses and take them home. The squire, who at his master's shout, left a group of friends and relatives he had among the crowd, a little red in the face, it must be said, walked over to the horses, skipping across a big pile of dung that had somehow formed at their feet; but no sooner had he reached out to take their halters to untie them than Master Himboldt, his cousin, stayed his hand and with the words: Don't you touch those knacker's mares! and he hurled him back from the cart. With that, Himboldt picked his way across the pile of dung and remarked to the Chamberlain, who stood there astounded at this turn of events: If he wanted such a service to be performed, he needed to engage an apprentice flayer! The Chamberlain, now foaming with rage, eyed Master Himboldt a moment, then turned, and over the heads of the knights ringing him, called for the guard; and no sooner had, on Wenk's command, an officer with a handful of the Elector's life guards issued from the castle than, giving him a brief account of the disgraceful meddling of the citizens, he ordered Master Himboldt, as their ringleader, to be placed under lock and key. Grabbing him by the shirt, he accused him of interfering with his squire who on his instructions was about to free the horses at the back of the cart, and violently throwing him down in the dirt. Master Himboldt, with an adroit movement freeing himself from the Chamberlain's grip, protested: Sir, telling a lad of twenty what to do is not inciting him to rebellion. Ask him yourself if he wants to get involved with the provenance and rightness of the horses that are tied to the cart; if he does, after what I've told him, then let him. For all I care he may as well flay them and skin them as well. Following these words, the Chamberlain turned to the young fellow and asked whether he had any objection to carrying out his instruction and freeing Kohlhaas's horses and taking them back to the house; and since the lad, shyly mingling with the citizenry, said: The horses have to be made honest horses before he could be expected to take a hand; then the Chamberlain approached him from behind, knocked the hat off his head that was decorated with his emblem, trampled it on the ground, took out his sword, and started thrashing him with the broad side of it, sending him fleeing from the square and his service. Master Himboldt cried out: Throw the murderous so-and-so to the floor! and while the indignant citizens surged forward, pushing the guards aside, he knocked the Chamberlain down from behind, pulled off his cloak, collar, and helmet, twisted the sword from his grip, and flung it across the square. In vain did the Junker Wenzel, fleeing from the affray, call out to the knights to assist his cousin; before they were able to take a single step they were already scattered by the crowd, leaving entirely at their mercy the Chamberlain who had taken a tumble and hurt his head. It took the appearance of a troop of mounted lansquenets that happened to cross the square, summoned to help by the life guards' officer, to rescue the Chamberlain. The officer, once he'd dispersed the crowd, picked up the furious Himboldt, and while he was escorted to prison by a couple of soldiers, two friends picked the unhappy, bloodied Chamberlain off the ground and took him home. Such was the calamitous conclusion of the honest and well-intentioned attempt to give the horse breeder redress for the wrong he had suffered. As the people began to melt away, the knacker of Döbbeln, whose business in town was done, and who had no desire to linger, tied the horses to a lamppost where they remained all day, to the mockery of urchins and ne'er-do-wells, till, as no one came forward to tend them, the police had to take them in hand, and towards nightfall, summoned the Dresden knacker to keep them in the knackery outside town till further notice.

This incident, however little the horse dealer had done to cause it, seemed nevertheless to rouse in the better sort and in moderate minds a very dangerous mood for the issue of his complaint. His relation to officialdom was found to be insupportable, and the sentiment was voiced in private homes and public places that it were better to inflict a manifest injustice on the man, and bring an end to the whole affair than to afford him justice, extorted by his violence, in such a nugatory matter, merely to the satisfaction of his inflexibility and rigid persistence. What led to the utter downfall of poor Kohlhaas was the fact that the Lord Chancellor himself, from an excess of right-mindedness and a consequent hatred of the Tronkas, ended up by contributing to this mood and spreading it further. It was most unlikely that the horses currently under the care of the Dresden flayer would ever be restored to the condition they had been in when they first left their stables at Kohlhaasenbrück. But even if it had been possible, by art and constant care, the humiliation that in these circumstances would have befallen the Junker's family was such that with their prominence in the state as one of the first and noblest families, nothing would have been easier and more practicable than to request a financial penalty in lieu. Nevertheless, upon receipt of a letter that the president, Count Kallheim, had written a few days later on behalf of the Chamberlain, who was still incapacitated by his injuries, making this very suggestion, the Lord Chancellor wrote to Kohlhaas, urging him, should he receive such an offer, not to dismiss it out of hand; but to the President himself, he wrote in brief, cool terms kindly not to burden him with private initiatives of this sort, urging the Chamberlain rather to apply directly to the horse dealer, whom he described as a quiet and biddable individual. The horse dealer, his will rather broken by what had transpired the other day in the market, was himself only waiting, in accordance with the advice of the Lord Chancellor, for some overture from the Junker's side to engage him with full goodwill and forgiveness for everything that had happened; yet, precisely such an overture was unforthcoming from the proud knights; embittered about the Lord Chancellor's reply, they showed it directly to the Elector when he called on his Chamberlain, lying abed with his wounds, on the morning of the following day. The Chamberlain, his voice weak and quavering, asked him if, having chanced his life in a bid to settle the affair in accordance with his wishes, he was still required to risk his honor to the censure of the world, and appear before a man who had brought all conceivable humiliation and disgrace upon his family with a plea for compromise. The Elector, having read the letter, now awkwardly asked Count Kallheim whether the Court didn't have the authority, without further application to Kohlhaas, to assert that the horses were beyond repair, and therefore go on to commute an eventual punishment to a financial penalty, just as though they had actually been dead? The Count replied: "Sir, they are dead; they are in legal terms dead, because they are of no value, and they will be physically dead by the time they have been taken out of the knackery and put in the knights' stables." Whereupon the Elector, pocketing the letter, said he would speak to his Lord Chancellor about the matter in person, allayed the anxious Chamberlain, who had pulled himself half-upright, and having urged him with warm insistence to look after himself, got out of his chair and left the room.

This was how things stood in Dresden when a second, more violent storm broke upon poor Kohlhaas, this time from Lützen, the buffets of which the canny knights were clever enough to direct upon his head. One Johann Nagelschmidt, one of the band of men assembled by the horse dealer and then, following the Elector's amnesty, disbanded again, had in his wisdom a few weeks later regrouped some of the band of criminals, and along the Bohemian border resumed on his own behalf the handiwork for which his time with Kohlhaas had given him a taste. Partly to strike fear in the legal officers on his trail, and partly as a means of encouraging the rural population to take up arms in his villainous enterprise, this wastrel was pleased to dub himself Kohlhaas's lieutenant. With a cleverness copied from his former leader, he put it about that the amnesty to several men who had quietly gone home had been broken, and Kohlhaas himself, in a breach of promise that cried to high heaven, had been arrested following his arrival in Dresden and was currently under guard. In posters whose style was modeled on Kohlhaas's, he portrayed his band of arsonists and thugs in the guise of an army set up for the grace of God, with the intention of supervising the promised amnesty. And all this, as said, not for the grace of God, nor out of loyalty to Kohlhaas, as to whose fate they were quite indifferent, but for a mask under which they might loot and burn to their hearts' desire. As soon as first news of this development reached Dresden, the knights were unable to conceal their joy at such a turn, which gave everything a new aspect. With grim and knowing sideways looks, they reminded one another of the mistake that had been made in ignoring their urgent and repeated warnings, and offering Kohlhaas an amnesty; it was really as though they purposed to encourage all sorts of criminals to follow in his footsteps; and not content with crediting Nagelschmidt's claim that he had taken up arms purely for the preservation and security of his immured chief, they expressed the conviction that this whole manifestation was nothing but a ruse initiated by Kohlhaas, to put fear into the government and win his expedited judgment point by point in accordance with his rampant self-will. Yes, the cupbearer, Hinz, went so far in the company of a few courtiers and falconers forgathered after board in the Elector's anteroom, as to depict the dissolution of the robber gang at Lützen as a damned charade; and while poking fun at the Lord Chancellor's love of justice, he went on to prove from various cleverly pieced together circumstances that the gang was still intact in the forests of the Electorate, and was merely awaiting a signal from the horse dealer to break out again with fire and sword. Prince Christian von Meissen, very unhappy about this turn of things, which threatened to blot the escutcheon of his master, straightaway went up to the castle to visit him; and, while seeing through the interest of the knights to plunge Kohlhaas to his doom on the basis of these new depredations, he nevertheless asked for leave to convene a hearing about

the horse dealer as soon as possible. The horse dealer, somewhat surprised, was brought to the palace by a constable, with
Heinrich and Leopold, his two sons in his arms; for Sternbald
the attendant had returned with his five little ones the day
before from Mecklenburg, where they had been staying, and
considerations of one kind or another to detail which would
take up too much space, prompted him to pick up the boys
who were crying hot childish tears at his departure and take
them with him to the hearing. The Prince, having benevo-
lently eyed the children whom Kohlhaas had sat down next
to him and graciously asking their names and ages, told him
what excesses his onetime subordinate Nagelschmidt had
permitted himself in the valleys of the Erz Mountains; and
letting him see the man's so-called manifestos, invited him to
bring forth anything he might have in his own defense. The
horse dealer, notwithstanding his horror at such shameful
and destructive documents, and even with a scrupulous man
like the Prince, had little trouble demonstrating the base-
lessness of the accusations against him to the latter's satisfaction. Not only that, as things stood, he claimed to need
no help from any third party in the resolution of his nicely
progressing legal affair; from some papers he was carrying
on his person and which he showed the Prince, it became
still less likely that the heart of a Nagelschmidt would be
inclined to do him any favors, because just a little before
disbanding his force at Lützen, he had been on the point of
hanging the fellow for rapine and sundry other crimes; so
that only the proclamation of the Elector's amnesty, dissev-
ering the relationship, had saved him, and the following day
the two had parted as deadly enemies. In accordance with the
Prince's suggestion, Kohlhaas sat down and wrote a public

letter to Nagelschmidt, in which he declared that any claim to have taken up arms on behalf of the allegedly broken amnesty for himself and his army was nothing but a shameful and scandalous lie; told him that on his arrival in Dresden he had been neither arrested, nor put under guard, and that his legal affair was progressing entirely satisfactorily; and warned the fellows around him that he, Nagelschmidt, faced the full vengeful force of the law for murders and arsons perpetrated in the Erz Mountains after publication of the amnesty. Attached to this were a few details relating to the criminal case the horse dealer had brought in the castle at Lützen concerning the aforementioned shameful events, included to educate the ordinary folk about this worthless, and even then gallows-bound fellow, who had only been saved at the eleventh hour by the Elector's intervention. The Prince put Kohlhaas at ease concerning the suspicion that inevitably, in view of the circumstances, had been voiced about him in this hearing. He assured him that so long as *he* was in Dresden, the amnesty would continue to obtain; shook hands with the two little boys, gave them some pieces of fruit from his table, saluted Kohlhaas and permitted him to leave. The Lord Chancellor, who well understood the peril the horse dealer was in, did his utmost to bring his affair to a conclusion before there could be any fresh complications; but that was precisely what the politic knights wished and sought to bring about, and instead of, as previously, silently admitting their culpability and limiting their information to a narrowly legalistic point of law, they now began with cunning and obstructive arguments to deny their guilt altogether. Now they claimed that Kohlhaas's horses had been detained at Tronkenburg through some initiative of the castellan and the steward, of which the Junker had been imperfectly informed;

now they swore that the animals had been sick with a violent and dangerous distemper when they had arrived, to which end they asked for witnesses to be brought in; and when they had been defeated in these arguments, following exhaustive investigations and confrontations, they then brought in an edict of the Elector's some dozen years old, that called for the import of horses from Brandenburg to Saxony to be stopped on account of a dangerous pestilence; this was clear proof that the Junker was not merely authorized but positively obliged to stop Kohlhaas's horses from crossing the frontier.

Kohlhaas, who by now had reacquired his farm at Kohlhaasenbrück from his stalwart neighbor the magistrate against a small penalty, now wished to leave Dresden and return home for a few days, it seemed, for official confirmation of this deal; a wish, we don't doubt, that was less to do with the transaction, however urgent it might be, and the sowing of winter corn, than a desire to reflect on his position under such remarkable and sinister circumstances; other reasons too may have played a part, which we will leave the individual reader to guess at. Accordingly, and leaving behind his appointed sentries, he called on the Lord Chancellor, and said to him, his neighbor's letter in hand, that he was minded, if as seemed likely he was not required in court, to leave the city and go home to Brandenburg for a week or two, at the end of which he undertook to return. The Lord Chancellor, looking at the ground with an ill-humored and thoughtful expression, replied: He had to admit that his presence was more essential now than ever, with the court requiring his evidence and explanations in view of the sophistical and cunning arguments of the other side, in a thousand unpredictable ways; but Kohlhaas, referring him to his thoroughly briefed lawyer, and with quiet persistence promising to confine himself to a single week, insisted on his wish, until finally, after a pause, the Lord Chancellor, in letting him go, said: "he hoped he would apply for a pass from Prince Christian von Meissen for the purpose."

Kohlhaas, expert by now at reading the expression of the Chancellor, sat down on the spot, reinforced in his resolve, and, without naming a reason, asked the Prince von Meissen, as acting head of the government, for a week's pass to Kohlhaasenbrück and back. By way of reply he received a note signed by the captain of the castle, Freiherr Siegfried von Wenk, confirming: "Your application for a pass to Kohlhaasenbrück will be put before the Elector for his approval, which as soon as it be obtained, the pass will be sent you." When Kohlhaas inquired of his lawyer why the palace's reply was signed by some Freiherr von Wenk, not by Prince Christian von Meissen, to whom he had applied, he was informed that the Prince had left for his country estates some three days ago, and that government business was being conducted in his absence by Freiherr von Wenk, the castle commander, a cousin of the gentleman referred to above.

Kohlhaas, whose heart began to beat a little unquietly with all these developments, spent several days waiting for his albeit casually presented petition to the Elector and then unaccountably passed on, to be answered; a week went by, and more, without news of the pass, nor yet with news of the outcome of his suit from the court, however confidently this too had been predicted; now, on the twelfth day, firmly resolved to flush out the position taken by the government towards him, whatever it might be, he sat down and asked the government once more for his passes, as a matter of urgency. How crestfallen he was, then, when on the evening of the following day, again without any answer, he walked thoughtfully over to the window of the little back room, in contemplation of his situation, and in particular of the amnesty that Doctor Luther had secured him, and for once failed to see in his place in the annex in the yard the sentry that the Prince of Meissen had ordered posted there on his arrival. Thomas, the old porter whom he summoned to him and asked what this was supposed to mean, replied with a sigh: Sir, things are not as they should be; the soldiers, of whom there are more today than usual, spread out all round the house at nightfall; there are two with spear and shield standing at the front door; two more at the garden gate; and another two lying in the anteroom on bundles of straw, declaring they mean to sleep there. Blenching, Kohlhaas turned away and remarked: "I wouldn't mind, so long as they were still there; and let him put out lanterns so that they would see him if he stepped outside." After opening one of the windows to the front, under pretext of emptying a chamber pot out into the street, he saw that what the old man had told him was indeed the case; because just then the guards were being silently relieved, which measure had no precedent: whereupon, though not tired in the least, he betook himself to bed, and his decision for the morrow had been taken. Because there was nothing that he took so much amiss from the government that he was involved with as the false appearance of justice, while they were in fact violating the terms of the amnesty they had offered him; and if he really was under house arrest, of which there could be little doubt, then he at least wanted from them the frank and unambiguous statement that this was the case. Accordingly, once the day had dawned, he had Sternbald the servant set the horses to his carriage, and draw it up to the door, so that, as he made known, he could drive out to his tenant farmer in Lockewitz, an old acquaintance, who had visited him in Dresden a few days prior, and invited him and his children to visit. The soldiers, noticing movements within and putting their heads together, secretly dispatched one of their number into the town, where within a few minutes a government official at the head of several police appeared, and, as though they had some business there, invested the house opposite. Kohlhaas, busy dressing his children, also observed this, and left the carriage outside the door longer than was strictly necessary, stepped outside the house with his children as soon as he saw the police had finished their preparations, all insouciantly, and while in passing he told the group of soldiers who were in front of the door that they had no need to follow him, he lifted the boys into the carriage and kissed and comforted his little crying daughters, who under his instructions, were to stay behind with the daughter of the old porter. No sooner had he climbed into the carriage himself than the government official with his suite of constables issued forth from the house opposite and asked him where he was going. To Kohlhaas's reply that "he was going to his friend in Lockewitz, who invited him and his sons a couple of days ago to visit him in the country," the official said that if this was the case he would have to wait a few moments for a detachment of mounted troops to accompany him, in accordance with the orders of the Prince of Meissen. Kohlhaas, smiling down from the carriage, asked: "Did he think he was unsafe at the house of a friend who had invited him to share his board for a day?" The officer replied in a droll and light-hearted manner that the danger did not strike him as excessively great; though he added that the men were not to be an encumbrance in any way. Kohlhaas replied earnestly: "that the Prince of Meissen on his arrival in Dresden left it at his discretion whether he wanted to use the guard or not." And since the official was surprised to learn this and used cautious expressions about the proper use of the guard during the whole duration of his stay in the city, the horse dealer told him about the incident that had led to the posting of a guard outside the house in the first place. The official assured him that the orders of the castle captain, Freiherr von Wenk, who was currently serving as chief of police had been to make the continual protection of his person a priority, and asked him, if he was unhappy about the escort, to go up to the palace to correct the misconception they must have about him up there. Kohlhaas, directing a speaking look at the official, and resolved to obtain certainty one way or another, said "he would do so," with pounding heart got out of the carriage, had the porter carry the boys back inside the house, and leaving groom and carriage waiting at the door, walked to the palace with the official and his men. It turned out that the castle commander, Freiherr von Wenk, was just busy questioning a group of Nagelschmidt's men who had been picked up in the Leipzig area the day before, and the fellows were being interrogated about several things they were curious to learn about by some knights who were with him when the horse dealer and his escort walked into the room. As soon as the horse dealer appeared, the knights suddenly went quiet and stopped their interrogation, and the Freiherr quickly walked over to him and asked what it was he wanted. And when the horse dealer had respectfully told him of his plan to lunch with the administrator at Lockewitz, and expressed the wish to leave behind the soldiers, whose presence he didn't require, the Freiherr replied, the color coming and going in his face, and seeming to bite back some other remark, "he would do well to stay quietly in his house, and for the time being put off the meal with the Lockewitz farmer."

With that von Wenk terminated the conversation, turned to the officer and said: "that there was a purpose for the order he gave him with respect to this man, and that he wasn't to leave the city except in the company of six mounted soldiers."

Kohlhaas asked if he was a prisoner then, and was he to think that the amnesty solemnly promised before all the world had been broken. To which the Freiherr suddenly flame-red in the face turned and stepping very close to him and staring him in the eye said Yes! Yes! Yes!—quickly turned his back on him and went back to the interrogation of the Nagelschmidt villains. Kohlhaas left the room, and though he understood that his only recourse, which was flight, had been made much more difficult by the steps he had taken, he was pleased nonetheless because now he felt on his side too that the obligations imposed on him by the terms of the amnesty didn't apply. When he got home, he had the horses taken out of harness, and accompanied by the official, feeling shaken and upset, went into his room. And while the man assured him in a way that was bound to seem rather repellent to the horse dealer that the whole thing must be based on a misunderstanding that would soon be resolved, the constables, at a wink from him, barred all the doors out into the courtyard; the official assured him that the front door remained, as before, his to use whenever he pleased.

In the meantime, in the forests of the Erz Mountains, Nagelschmidt was being pressed on all sides by constables and soldiers, so that in his helplessness and desperation at being unable to fulfill the sort of role he had taken over, he thought of making a genuine appeal to Kohlhaas; and getting from a traveler walking the highway a fairly accurate representation of the current state of his legal affair in Dresden, he supposed, that for all the purported enmity between them he might be able to persuade the horse dealer to enter into a new compact with him. Accordingly, he dispatched a squire to him with a barely literate letter, the gist of which was: "If you are willing to come to Altenburg and take over the command of the troop which consists of remnants of your old force, then he offered to help him escape from his incarceration in Dresden with men, horses, and money. He promised furthermore to be more obedient, and more orderly and just better than before, and as proof of his fealty and affection was even now setting off for the environs of Dresden, to assist in his liberation." Now the fellow to whom this letter had been entrusted, in a village just outside Dresden, suffered the misfortune of being struck down with painful cramps to which he had been a martyr from boyhood; in the course of which the letter, which he was carrying in a pouch around his neck, was found by the persons who came to his aid, and he himself, as soon as he was improved, was arrested, and transported to the palace under guard, and accompanied by a throng of people. No sooner had the commander von Wenk read the letter than he went directly to the castle, where he found Messrs Hinz and Kunz (the first of them now recovered from his wounds), and the President of the Chancellery, Count Kallheim, in attendance. The gentlemen were of the mind that Kohlhaas should be arrested forthwith and made to stand trial on the basis of his secret agreement with Nagelschmidt; they intended to prove that such a letter could not have been written without antecedents from the horse dealer's hand, and without there being a vicious criminal conspiracy between the two men planning a campaign of fresh atrocities. The Elector steadfastly refused, on the basis of this letter, to violate the conditions of the free pass he had offered; Nagelschmidt's letter suggested to him that there was actually no prior understanding between them; and all he would agree to do, to find out how things stood, was, after long hesitation, accept the President's suggestion, and allow the letter to be delivered by Nagelschmidt's fellow as if he had never been apprehended, and see if it got an answer. The squire, then, who had been thrown in prison, was brought to the palace the following morning, where the commander returned the letter to him, and assuring him he was free, and the punishment he merited had been served, told him to deliver the letter to the horse dealer, as though nothing had befallen. The fellow agreed to this bad trick without further ado, and with much show of secrecy, under guise of having crabs to sell, with which the official had furnished him from the market, he entered Kohlhaas's room. While the children played with the crabs, Kohlhaas read the letter; under other circumstances he would have taken the fellow by the scruff of the neck and delivered him to the soldiers who stood outside; but since, to his current state of feeling, even such a step was capable of a cynical interpretation, and he had convinced himself that nothing in the world could spring him from the situation in which he found himself, so he looked at the fellow's familiar face with a sad expression, asked him where he lived, and promised to give him his decision regarding his master in a few more hours, here. He told Sternbald, who happened to walk in, to buy the man's crabs, and after that was done, and both had gone out again, not having recognized one another, he sat down and wrote a letter to Nagelschmidt, as follows: "First of all, that he accepts the offer concerning the command of his troop in Altenburg; that he should send a carriage with two horses to Dresden Neustadt, to free him and his five children from the detention they are being held in; that he would need a further pair of horses on the highway to Wittenberg to make good his escape, alone, and for reasons that were too complicated to bear telling; that he thought he could corrupt the lansquenets who were guarding him by a bribe, but in case violence was required, the presence of a couple of doughty bold and well-armed fellows in Neustadt would be helpful; that for the carrying out of all these measures he was sending him a roll of twenty pieces of gold with the messenger, and expected him to be able to account for them afterwards; that he asked him not to come to Dresden, because that was unnecessary, yes, that he went so far as to give him the strict command to stay with his men in Altenburg, and not leave them leaderless."

This, then, was the letter he gave the man when he came again towards evening; he paid him well and told him to take care of the letter.

It was his plan to go to Hamburg with his five little ones, and from there to take ship for the Levant or the East Indies, or anywhere with a blue sky and strange people, because his battered spirit had abandoned the idea of feeding the horses, quite apart from his unwillingness to make common cause with Nagelschmidt.

No sooner had the messenger taken this letter to the commander than the Lord Chancellor was dismissed, the President, Count Kallheim, promoted to his place as head of the Tribunal, and Kohlhaas officially detained by command of the Elector, placed under arrest, and brought up to the tower laden with chains. He was charged on the basis of the letter, copies of which were put up all over the city, and when the lawyer asked him in court whether he recognized the handwriting, he replied "Yes!" but when asked if he had anything to say on his own behalf he lowered his gaze, replied "No!"

and was sentenced to be pincered with red-hot irons by torturers, quartered, and his body burned between wheel and gallows.

This was how things stood for poor Kohlhaas in Dresden when the Elector of Brandenburg appeared to rescue him from the hands of arbitrary power, and in a note delivered to the Saxon Chancellery, claimed him for one of his subjects. For the good Mayor, Heinrich von Geusau, had told him, in the course of a stroll along the banks of the River Spree, the story of this unusual and far from contemptible man, in the course of which, in answer to questions from the astonished ruler, he couldn't avoid mentioning the blame that attached to the Chancellor, Siegfried, Count Kallheim, and hence implicated the Elector of Brandenburg himelf; whereupon the monarch, deeply upset, summoned Kallheim and found that his consanguinity with the Tronkas was to blame for everything, dismissed him with many signs of disfavor, and appointed Heinrich von Geusau in his place.

It so happened, however, that the Polish crown, at odds with the Elector of Saxony over we know not what matters, made urgent and repeated application to the Elector of Brandenburg, to enter into an alliance against the Saxons; and the Chancellor Geusau, not inexpert in such affairs, entertained hope that he might be able to fulfill the wish of his friend Kohlhaas, cost what it may, for justice, without risking the stability of the generality more than regard for an individual might warrant. The Chancellor demanded the immediate and unconditional release of Kohlhaas, not merely for the arbitrary nature of the proceedings against him—offensive to God and man alike—promising that, if he were guilty, he would face trial under the laws of Brandenburg, with the case against him being brought by an attorney in Berlin on the basis of a suit drawn up by the court in Dresden; he even ordered passes for a lawyer the Elector was willing to send to Dresden, to obtain justice for Kohlhaas over the horses that had been taken from him on Saxon soil and sundry other maltreatment and acts of violence that had been unconscionably perpetrated against him by the Junker Wenzel von Tronka. The Chamberlain, Kunz, who had been promoted to President of the Chancellery in the recent reallocation of posts in Saxony, and who had several reasons not to offend the Court at Berlin in the pickle in which he found himself, replied on behalf of his very depressed superior on receipt of this note: "that we are surprised at the unfriendliness and brazenness with which the court at Dresden is denied the right to try Kohlhaas for crimes committed in our country and by our own laws, since it is very widely known he even owns a considerable piece of property in our capital, and does not deny himself to be a Saxon subject." But since the Polish crown was assembling an army five thousand strong along the borders of Saxony to support its claims in their dispute, and the Chancellor, Heinrich von Geusau declared: "that Kohlhaasenbrück, the place that gives the horse dealer his name, is situated in Brandenburg, and that we would view the execution of the death penalty on him as a violation of international law," so the Elector on the advice of his Chamberlain Kunz, no less, who sought to withdraw from these complications, recalled Prince Christian von Meissen from his estates, and decided, after a few words from this sensible gentleman, to hand over Kohlhaas to the Berlin courts as requested. The Prince, who, though not best pleased with the course taken by events, at the desire of his hard-pressed monarch, was forced to take charge of the Kohlhaas affair, inquired why proceedings were now to be advanced against Kohlhaas in Berlin, and since they didn't want to refer to the Nagelschmidt letter on account of the doubtful circumstances of its writing, nor could they adduce the previous plunderings and burnings on account of the paper in which it was declared that he had been forgiven for them, therefore the Elector resolved to show His Majesty the Emperor in Vienna a report on Kohlhaas's armed rampagings in Saxony, to complain at his breach of the Emperor's public order, and urge that His Imperial Majesty, not being bound by any amnesty, have the case against Kohlhaas pursued by an Imperial lawyer at the courts in Berlin. A week later, the horse dealer, in chains, was transported by the knight Friedrich von Malzahn whom the Brandenburg Elector had sent with an escort of six men down to Dresden, loaded onto a carriage, and, with his five children who at his beseeching had been traced to various orphanages and foundling homes, conveyed back to Berlin. As luck would have it, the Elector of Saxony, at the invitation of the District Prefect, Aloysius Count Kallheim, who owned property in the Saxon marches, in the society of his Chamberlain Kunz, and the latter's wife, Lady Heloise, daughter of the Prefect and sister of the President, and many other glittering gentlemen and ladies, hunting Junkers and courtiers, had assembled for a great stag hunt, that, to amuse the monarch was being held at Dahme; the whole society, still mantled with dust from the chase, attended by pages and noble youths, to the sound of cheery music being performed around the trunk of an oak, were sitting at table under the roofs of wimpled pavilions erected on a hillside on both sides of the highway, just as the horse dealer and his escort passed slowly along the road from Dresden. For one of the delicate little Kohlhaases had fallen ill, forcing Malzahn to stop for three days at Herzberg, which necessity he, who owed allegiance only to his own ruler, had not seen fit to communicate to the government at Dresden. The Elector, with shirt unbuttoned, his feathered hat trimmed in hunting style with fir twigs, sitting by the side of Lady Heloise, who, many years earlier, had been his paramour, said, in the cheer brought on by the pleasant feeling of the party around him: "Let us go down and bring the unhappy man, whoever he may be, a bumper of wine!" Lady Heloise, darting him an affectionate look, straightaway stood up, and taking from the whole table, heaped a silver tray a page handed her with bread, cake, and fruit; and the whole party had swarmed out of the pavilion with refreshments of all sorts, when the Prefect walked up to them with sheepish expression, and asked them to stop a moment. To the apprehensive question of the Elector what the matter might be to make him so awkward, the Prefect replied, stammering in the direction of the Chamberlain, that the person in the carriage was Kohlhaas; to which stunning piece of news—the whole world knew he had left fully a week ago—the Chamberlain, Herr Kunz, picked up his goblet of wine and turning back towards the pavilion, emptied it into the sand. The Elector, blushing furiously, set down his own on a platter a noble boy came rushing up to him with, at a nod from the Chamberlain; and while Friedrich von Malzahn, respectfully greeting the company, whom he did not know, slowly moved on through the tents that ran across the highway, in the direction of Dahme, the company, at the invitation of the Prefect, betook themselves back into their tent. As soon as the Elector had seated himself, the Prefect sent a discreet message to Dahme, to have the magistrate there expedite, if possible, the further transport of the horse dealer; but since the man, in view of the lateness of the hour, said he would have to spend the night there, they had to content themselves with silently accommodating him in a farm belonging to the magistrate, to the side of the highway behind bushes. Now it transpired that towards evening, when the company diverted by wine and the enjoyment of plentiful desserts, had forgotten the entire incident, the Prefect thought to lie in wait again, because a stag herd had put in an appearance; which suggestion the entire company joyfully took up, and in pairs taking up guns, they swarmed over ditches and hedges into the nearby forest; so that the Elector and Lady Heloise—who, to view the spectacle, hung on his arm—were led by a squire, to their astonishment through the yard of the farm where Kohlhaas and the Brandenburg troop had been put up. The lady, hearing this, said: "Come along, sir, come!" and playfully concealing the chain he wore round his neck in his silken shirt, "let us go and hide in the farm before the hunters return, and see for ourselves the strange man who is staying there!" The Elector, blushing, and taking her hand, said, Heloise, how can you? But since, looking at him awkwardly, she replied "that no one would recognize him in his huntsman's garb!" and dragged him on; and at just that moment, a couple of hunting junkers, having already satisfied their curiosity, emerged from the house, telling one another that, thanks to the precautions taken by the Prefect, neither the knight nor the horse dealer knew what company was in the vicinity of Dahme; then the Elector laughingly pulled his hat down over his eyes, and said: "Folly, you rule the world, and your preferred seat is the shapely mouth of a woman!"

As luck would have it, Kohlhaas was sitting on a heap of straw with his back to the wall, feeding bread and milk to the child of his that had fallen ill at Herzberg, when the company who would fain visit him stepped into the farm, and when the lady, opening the conversation inquired who he was, and what ailed the child, also what crime had he committed and where was he being taken with such an escort? so that he took off his leather cap, and carrying on with what he was doing, gave brief but satisfactory replies to her questions. The Elector, standing behind the hunting junkers, noticing a small lead cylinder hanging from the man's neck on a silken thread, asked him, for want of other entertainment what that might be, and what was in it? Kohlhaas replied: "Indeed, sir, this cylinder!"—and he slipped it off, opened it, and took out a small piece of paper sealed with wax—"this cylinder is a rare thing! It was seven months ago, the day after my wife's burial, and as you may know, I had set out from Kohl-haasenbrück, to capture the Junker von Tronka, who had done me considerable wrong, when, for some negotiation of which I have no knowledge, the Electors of Saxony and Brandenburg met in Jüterbog, a market town through which I happened to be passing; and since towards evening they had come to an agreement, they were walking in friendly conversation through the streets of the town to inspect a fair that was just then being held. There they encountered a gypsy woman sitting on a stool, from a star chart telling the fortunes of people who were besieging her, and the two rulers asked her lightheartedly, whether she didn't happen to have some news for them as well? I, having just put up with my men at an inn, was present where this was happening; I stood at the entrance of a church, unable to hear through the dense crowd what the weird woman was telling the gentle-men; people were laughing and whispering to one another that she wouldn't share her knowledge with just anyone, and they thronged to get closer so as not to miss the story, while

I, less curious, in fact more to make room for the onlookers, happened to climb up on a stone bench in the entrance to the church. No sooner was I installed on my vantage point looking at the gentlemen and the gypsy woman sitting in front of them on her stool appearing to write something down, than she suddenly stands up, leans on her two crutches and stares out into the crowd; she fixes me—who had never spoken a word to her, and never in my life wanted anything to do with her science—and forces her way through the dense crowd to me, saying: 'There! If the gentleman seeks to know, then let him ask thee!' And with that, sir, she passed me this scrap of paper here with her bony hand. And while, disconcerted as you may imagine as all eyes are upon me, I protest, little mother, what is this you are favoring me with? She replies, along with a lot of gobbledygook among which I happen to my great dismay to hear my own name: 'An amulet, Kohlhaas, horse dealer; look after it well, and it will one day save your life!' and she disappears."

"So," Kohlhaas cheerfully concluded: "to tell the truth, it didn't cost me my life in Dresden, though it was a close-run thing; and as to whether I fare any better with it in Berlin, time will tell."

At these words the Elector sat down on a bench; and answering the lady's concerned question, was anything amiss with him, he replied: Nothing, nothing at all! and, so saying, fell unconscious to the floor, before she had a chance to leap up and take him in her arms. The knight von Malzahn, happening to walk into the room on some errand, exclaimed: Good God! What is the matter? The lady cried: Bring water! The hunting junkers picked him up and carried him into a bed in the next room; and consternation reached a climax when the Chamberlain, summoned by a page boy, after several vain attempts to bring him back to life, declared: He shows every sign of having had an apoplexy! The Prefect, the cupbearer having sent a mounted messenger to Luckau to fetch a doctor, had the Elector brought to a carriage the minute he opened his eyes, and they went off at a slow pace to a hunting lodge he owned in the area; but even after he arrived, the journey provoked two further fits of unconsciousness, so that it wasn't until late the following morning when the surgeon arrived from Luckau, that he was somewhat revived, albeit with symptoms of an impending nervous fever. As soon as he had recovered his wits, he half sat up in bed, and his first question was: Where was Kohlhaas? The Chamberlain, misunderstanding his purpose, took his hand and said that he could set his mind at rest in that regard, the appalling individual, following that strange and baffling incident at the farm in Dahme, had remained behind under Brandenburg escort. He asked, assuring him of his liveliest sympathy and promising that he had severely upbraided his wife for her folly in bringing him together with this individual: What in their conversation had been so disturbing? The Elector said he had to admit that the sight of a scrap of paper that the man was carrying in a lead cartridge about his neck was to blame for the entire disagreeable turn. He went on speaking about this circumstance, in terms that were baffling to the Chamberlain; abruptly assuring him, clasping the Chamberlain's hand in his, that the possession of the paper was of the utmost importance to him; and asked him to saddle up on the spot and ride to Dahme and obtain the paper, quite regardless of what it cost. The Chamberlain, with difficulty concealing his consternation, assured him that if the paper was of such value for him, nothing in the world were more important than keeping this fact from Kohlhaas;

for as soon as some incautious remark made him aware of it, not all the wealth he had in the world would be sufficient to buy it from the hands of this unappeasable and vindictive fellow. He added, to soothe him a little, that they should think of some other way of getting at it, perhaps a stratagem involving some innocent third party as cat's-paw, as the villain in all probability didn't care for the thing for its own sake, and it might be possible to extract it from him. The Elector, mopping his brow, asked if they shouldn't send to Dahme right away, and delay the onward progress of the horse dealer till they had managed by one way or another to get the paper in their possession? The Chamberlain, not believing his ears, replied that presumably the horse dealer would have left Dahme by now, and would find himself on the other side of the frontier, on Brandenburg soil, where any attempt to delay, let alone reverse, his progress would encounter severe, even insuperable difficulties. He asked, as the Elector silently threw himself back onto his pillows in the attitude of one giving up all hope, what was on the paper? And through what strange and inexplicable chance was it known to him that its contents regarded himself? This time, however, with doubtful looks at the Chamberlain, whose eagerness to oblige he didn't in this case entirely trust, the Elector made no reply. He lay there rigid, with restless, pounding heart, seeming to stare at the corner of his lace handkerchief he was holding pressed in both hands, seemingly lost in thought, and abruptly asked him to call in the hunting Junker von Stein, a young, vigorous, and practical gentleman of whose services he had often availed himself in various confidential matters, under the pretext that he had some other business to discuss with him. After telling the hunting Junker the story, and informing him of the importance of the paper in Kohlhaas's possession, the Elector asked von Stein whether he was interested in gaining his immortal friendship, and acquiring the paper before Kohlhaas reached Berlin? And when von Stein, once he had a grasp of the situation, extraordinary though it was, assured him that he was entirely at his service, then the Elector instructed him to follow Kohlhaas on horseback, and, since money probably wouldn't influence him, to contrive a meeting and offer him life and liberty for it, yes, even, should he insist, support him right away, albeit with all due caution, with horses, men, and money, to get away from the troop of Brandenburgers who were escorting him. Von Stein, having asked for a handwritten note from the Elector to confirm his mission, then set off immediately with several men, and not sparing the horses, was fortunate enough to catch up with Kohlhaas in a border village, where, with his five children and the escorting Malzahn, he was lunching in the open outside the doors of a cottage. Introducing himself to Malzahn as a stranger on his way through, and curious to take a peek at the unusual prisoner, Malzahn readily invited him to join the table, and made him acquainted with Kohlhaas. And since the knight was coming and going, busy with preparations, while the soldiers were eating at a separate table on the other side of the house, there was an early opportunity for von Stein to make himself known to the horse dealer and explain the nature of his particular business. The horse dealer, already knowing the name and rank of the man whom the sight of the cartridge in the farmhouse at Dahme had caused to lose consciousness, and needing nothing to crown his own joyful agitation but possibly a look at the secret entrusted to the piece of paper, which, for several reasons he was resolved not to open for mere curiosity's sake: the horse dealer said, in view of the ignoble and ungenerous treatment he had received at Dresden, in spite of his own willingness to compromise in every way imaginable, that "he wanted to keep the paper." To the Junker's question what prompted him to make such an extraordinary refusal, in view of the fact that he was being offered life and liberty for it, Kohlhaas replied: "Noble sir! If your ruler were to come to me and say, I am prepared to destroy myself and the whole court of those that maintain me in power—destroy, you understand, which is the greatest wish I have in my heart: then I would still refuse him the paper that is worth more than his existence and say: You can take me to the scaffold if you like, but I can hurt you, and I will!" And with that, looking grim as death, he called a soldier telling him there was a goodly portion of food still left in the dish, and he should have it, and for the rest of the hour he spent in that little place he was as though absent to the Junker, and only turned to him as he boarded the carriage with a look of farewell.

The condition of the Elector, upon hearing this news, worsened to the degree that for three critical days the doctor feared for his life that seemed to be under simultaneous attack from so many different quarters. Finally, after several weeks spent in his sickbed, and thanks only to the strength of his constitution, he was restored at least sufficiently that they could put him in a carriage with pillows and blankets and transport him back to the seat of government at Dresden. As soon as he was back in the city, he summoned Prince Christian von Meissen and asked him how things stood with the briefing of Councillor Eibenmayer, whom they intended to send to Vienna as the prosecutor to present the case against Kohlhaas for breach of the Imperial peace. The Prince replied that in accordance with instructions left before the Elector had set off for Dahme, just after the arrival of Zäuner, whom the Elector of Brandenburg had sent as his attorney to Dresden to plead his case against Junker Wenzel von Tronka over the horses, the man had left for Vienna. The Elector, blushing, walked up to his desk, a little irked by so much haste, because so far as he knew he had left matters so that he wanted to give Eibenmayer some more detailed and precise instructions before sending him off, to which end he also wanted to have another conversation with Doctor Luther who had elaborated the amnesty. Unhappily, and barely managing to stifle his dissatisfaction, he heaped up various papers and files on his desk. The Prince, after a pause in which he merely looked on, remarked that he was sorry if he had occasioned the Elector's displeasure in the matter; but he could show him the decision of the Cabinet charging him with dispatching the lawyer at the time indicated. He added that in the Cabinet there had been no mention of further conversations with Doctor Luther; this might have been of advantage earlier, to consult the priest over the role he had assigned to Kohlhaas, but that wasn't the case now that they had violated the amnesty in full sight of all the world, arrested the man, and had him packed off to Brandenburg for sentencing and punishment. The Elector said the regrettable fact that they had sent Eibenmayer off already didn't greatly matter; but he would wish the man not to take up his role as prosecutor in Vienna for the time being, and asked the Prince to have an express messenger sent there to inform him thusly. The Prince answered that this order was unfortunately a day late, a report had come in today detailing how he had appeared as an attorney and had proceeded to make his case before the Court at Vienna. To the Elector's stricken question: How was this possible in so short a time? he replied that three weeks had passed already since the man's departure, and that the instruction he had received had charged him with the finishing of this business forthwith, straight after his arrival in Vienna. A delay, remarked the Prince, would have been the more regrettable in this instance as the Brandenburg lawyer Zäuner was proceeding against Wenzel von Tronka with the grimmest dispatch, and had already applied for a provisional injunction before the court, taking the horses from the flayer's hands, to have them readied for subsequent restoration of health, notwithstanding all the arguments of the defense. The Elector, pulling the bell, said: "Never mind that. It means nothing!" and after returning to the Prince, asking variously what had happened during his absence? And anything else? Unable to mask his inner agitation, he let him go with a handshake. That same day the Elector asked him in writing for all the files in the Kohlhaas case, claiming that the affair had become so politically important that he wanted to take personal charge of it. And since the thought that he was destroying the man from whom alone he might hope to learn the secrets of the scrap of paper was so unbearable to him, he addressed a personal letter to the Emperor, asking him urgently and warmly for important reasons that he might be able to tell him about later, for the time being to rescind the charge that Eibenmayer had submitted against Kohlhaas. The Emperor, in a note drawn up by his department of chancellery, replied: "That this sudden change of heart rather surprised him; that the report from the Saxon Electorate had made the Kohlhaas affair a matter for the entire Holy Roman Empire; that accordingly, he as the Emperor and overlord of the whole had seen himself called upon to argue the case before the house of Brandenburg; that the attorney Franz Müller had gone to Berlin in his capacity as Imperial advocate to obtain justice from Kohlhaas for breach of the public peace, and the complaint could not now be retracted, and in accordance with the laws, would take its further progress." The receipt of this letter crushed the Elector; and since, to his extreme distress letters came from spies in Berlin, reporting on the initiation of proceedings there, and it was declared that in all probability, notwithstanding the efforts of the defense, Kohlhaas would end on the scaffold: so the unhappy Elector decided to make one more attempt, and he pleaded with the Elector of Brandenburg in a note from his own hand to spare the life of the horse dealer. He claimed that the amnesty that had been offered the fellow necessarily did not permit of a sentence of death for him; assured him that in spite of the seeming severity with which he was proceeding against him, it had never been his intention to have the man die; and he described to the Elector how wretched he would feel if the protection he had offered him in Berlin should finally, and unexpectedly, turn out to be of greater disadvantage to him than if he had remained in Dresden, and had his case decided under Saxon law. The Brandenburg Elector, to whom much of this seemed unclear and ambiguous, replied: "That the dispatch with which the lawyer for the Imperial side is proceeding quite simply did not permit him to leave the straight path of the law, as he had desired." He observed that the concerns advanced to him went too far, in that the complaint before the Court in Berlin regarding the crimes for which the amnesty had been issued, did not come from him, the issuer of the amnesty, but rather from the Emperor himself, who was not a party to it. He would furthermore argue that, in view of the continuing violence of Nagelschmidt, whose campaign of terrorism had with extraordinary brazenness now been extended to Brandenburg territory, it was essential to present a deterrent example, and he asked him should he want to have all this set aside, then to make appeal to the Emperor in person, because if there were to be a decision in Kohlhaas's favor, it could only come from that quarter. The Elector, angered and frustrated by so much failure, was promptly stricken down again, and when his Chamberlain visited him one morning, the Elector showed him copies of letters he had sent to the courts of Vienna and Berlin, in an effort at least to extend the life of Kohlhaas and hence win time to acquire control of the scrap of paper that was in his possession. The Chamberlain fell to his knees before his monarch and begged him by all that was holy and precious, to tell him what was contained on the scrap of paper. The Elector told him to bolt the door, and sit down at his bedside; and after clasping his hand and, sighing, pressing it to his heart, he began: "Your wife, I believe, has already told you how the Elector of Brandenburg and I, on the third day of our meeting in Jüterbog, met a gypsy woman; and the Elector, being an enlightened fellow, decided to have a little fun with her reputation with a joke in front of the public, because her abilities were being celebrated at table excessively: therefore with arms crossed he stepped up to her table and, in relation to a prophesy she was to make regarding him, asked to have some token of her skill that could be confirmed that very day, because otherwise he said he wouldn't believe a word she said, though she were the Sibyl of Rome herself. The woman, eyeing us from head to toe, said the sign would be as follows: the great horned deer that the gardener's son was raising in the park would come to meet us in the marketplace before we were gone from there. Now you must know, this deer, which is destined for the table in Dresden, is kept in a fenced enclosure, under the shadow of great oaks, and behind lock and key, with other, smaller poultry and game creatures, and that the park and the gardens beyond, are all securely locked, so that it was impossible to imagine how the creature, as had strangely been promised us, would come to meet us where we were; nevertheless, fearing some sort of trick, the Elector, after briefly discussing it with me, decided to preclude for good and all everything that might yet happen, and ordered to have the deer killed forthwith and served up on the morrow. Thereupon he turned to the gypsy woman before whom all this was proposed out loud, and he said: Well now, what do you see in my future? The woman, looking at his hand, said: Hail, Elector and ruler! Your grace will reign for a long time, the house from which you come will continue for a long time, and your heirs will be great and magnificent, and will achieve power beyond all the lords and rulers of the earth! The Elector looked thoughtfully at the woman, said half-aloud with a step in my direction that he was almost sorry to have sent a messenger with his instructions to destroy the prophesy; and while money rained from the hands of his retinue onto the lap of the woman, much to the general delight, he asked her, reaching into his purse himself and adding a piece of gold: Whether her news for me was as ringing as was the case with him? The woman opened a chest by her side, and painstakingly and elaborately stowed away the money in it, locked it again, hid her hand from the sun, as though it bothered her, and looked at me; and when I repeated my question, she examined my palm, and I remarked to the Elector: It looks like she doesn't have such good tidings for *me*. Then she picked up her crutches, slowly raised herself off her stool, pressed herself close to me, and cupping her hands, whispered distinctly in my ear: No!

"I see, I said in confusion, and took a step back from her, as she returned to her stool, her eyes cold and inert, like marble. Then, I asked, from what quarter is the peril for my house? The woman, taking a piece of charcoal and paper, asked if she should write it down for me? And, unhappily, since the circumstances left me no other option, I replied: Yes! Do so. And she replied: 'Very well, I will write down three things for you: the name of the last ruler in your family, the date he loses his kingdom, and the name of the one who with force of arms will take it over.' Having settled this in front of the watching populace, she gets up, closes the paper with wax that she breathes on with her wizened mouth, and seals it with a lead sealing ring she wears on her middle finger. And as I am reaching for the paper, more curious than words can say, she suddenly says: 'No, Your Majesty,' and she turns and she picks up one of her crutches: 'go to that man there with the feathered hat standing on the bench behind all the people at the entrance to the church and pick up the paper if you like!' And then, before I have properly grasped what is going on, she leaves me standing in the square speechless with astonishment; and while she packs up the chest behind her, and takes it under her arm, she melts away into the crowd, without my being able to follow her. Now, to my not inconsiderable comfort, at that very moment the knight whom the Elector had dispatched to his castle turned up and reported with a laugh that the deer had been killed and dragged into the kitchen before his eyes by a couple of huntsmen. The Elector, smartly linking arms with mine, meaning to lead me away from the square, said: Well then! That prophesy was a cheap trick, hardly worthy of our time and money. How great then was our astonishment when, before he had even finished speaking, a shout rang up in the square, and all eyes were turned to a large butcher's dog trotting along from the castle, where he had grabbed the deer by the scruff and made off with it, and, followed by servants and maids, dropped the animal not three paces from us. It was as the gypsy woman had prophesied and seemed to lend validity to everything else she had foretold: the deer, albeit dead, had come to meet us in the market. A bolt of lightning dropping from heaven on a winter's day could not have had more deadly effect than that sight, and my first endeavor, as soon as I was freed from the society in which I found myself, was to look for the man with the feather hat whom the gypsy woman had indicated to me; but not one of my people sent out on that mission for three days was able to give me the least news of him. And now, Kunz my friend, I saw the man just a few weeks ago, in the farm at Dahme with my own eyes."

And with that he relinquished the hand of the Chamberlain, and mopping his brow, fell back into bed. The Chamberlain, to whom it seemed a waste of effort to oppose his master's view of the incident with his own, asked him to consider some method of obtaining the paper, and then leaving the fellow to his fate. But the Elector answered straight out that he could see no way, even though the very notion of losing the paper, and letting its secret knowledge go to the grave with the man brought him close to despair. To his friend's question, had he tried to find the gypsy woman? the Elector replied that the government, on a spurious order he had given, was to this day seeking her in all the open places of the Electorate; even though, for reasons he didn't care to elaborate, he suspected she wasn't even in Saxony. It now transpired that the Chamberlain, on account of several substantial properties in the Neumark that his wife had inherited from the former and now deceased Lord Chancellor, Count Kallheim, needed to travel to Berlin. After brief reflection, he asked the Elector, to whom he was deeply devoted, would he allow him a free hand there to pursue the matter? and since the Elector, pressing his hand to his heart, answered: "Be as though you were I, and procure the paper for me!" at which the Chamberlain made arrangements concerning his other business, brought forward the date of his departure by a few days, and, leaving his wife behind, left for Berlin on his own, with a few attendants.

Kohlhaas, by now, as stated, already in Berlin, and brought on special orders of the Brandenburg Elector to confined quarters that housed him and his five children in relative comfort, had immediately on the arrival of the Imperial lawyer from Vienna, been arraigned before the court on the charge of having disturbed the public order of the Empire; and even though he countered by saying that his campaign in Saxony, and associated acts of violence, were not subject to further justice, since the accommodation reached at Lützen with the Elector of Saxony; but he was informed that His Majesty the Emperor, whose lawyer was arraigning him, was unable to pay any regard to that arrangement; and when he had the case explained to him, and learned, that, differently to Saxony, he was here assured of a satisfactory outcome to his proceedings against the Junker Wenzel von Tronka, he felt perfectly content. It then happened, that on the very day of the Chamberlain's arrival, the court was deciding the case, and he was sentenced to death by beheading; a judgment no one, given the complicated state of the legal case, quite irrespective of its mildness, believed would be carried out, yes, that the whole city, in view of the affection the Brandenburg

Elector had for Kohlhaas, hoped to see commuted by fiat to a long and arduous prison sentence. The Chamberlain, seeing there was no time to waste if the assignment given him by his master was to be fulfilled, began his efforts by showing himself demonstratively and in full court attire to Kohlhaas, as he was standing at his window one morning, harmlessly looking out at the passersby. Then, concluding by a sudden movement of the man's head that Kohlhaas had seen him, noting especially to his intense satisfaction that the horse dealer's hand involuntarily reached to his chest to touch the amulet, he took what had happened in the man's soul for sufficient encouragement to take the next step towards the acquisition of the paper.

The Chamberlain summoned an ancient crone who went around on crutches, selling junk in the Berlin streets, whom he had made out among a gaggle of other such figures that dealt in rags, and whom in age and garb he took to correspond fairly well with the person the Elector had described. And assuming that Kohlhaas wouldn't have memorized the features of the woman who in their fleeting encounter gave him the paper, he decided to put her forward in place of the other and have her play the part of the gypsy woman to Kohlhaas, if possible. To prepare her, he told her everything that had transpired between the Elector and the gypsy woman in Jüterbog, laying particular emphasis—because he wasn't sure how far the woman had gone in her speech to Kohlhaas— on the three particulars itemized on the piece of paper. And after briefing her what she had to let fall, incoherently and vaguely, in accordance with certain plans that had been made, towards the obtaining, either by cunning or by main force, of the piece of paper that was of such importance to the Saxon ruler, he told her to demand the paper from Kohlhaas under the pretext that it was no longer safe with him, to keep it for a few decisive days herself. The rag and bone woman was offered the prospect of a substantial reward, of which the Chamberlain, at her demand, was forced to pay down a portion in advance, and duly accepted the task. And since the mother of Kohlhaas's squire Herse fallen at Mühlberg from time to time came to visit him, and the beggar woman had known her for several months, she was able on one of the following days, by means of a small bribe to the jailer, to gain admission to the horse dealer's lodgings.

When the woman walked in, Kohlhaas thought by a seal ring she wore on her hand and a dangling string of corals round her neck he recognized the gypsy woman who had handed him the paper in Jüterbog. And just as verisimilitude and fact are not always perfectly aligned, something happened next that we will report, but permit readers who prefer to doubt it to doubt. When choosing a woman off the streets to impersonate the gypsy woman the Chamberlain had made the colossal mistake of choosing none other than the mysterious gypsy woman herself. Be that as it may, the woman, propping herself up on her crutches, and dandling the cheeks of the children, who, alarmed by her strange appearance, clustered round their father, reported that she had returned from Saxony to Brandenburg some time ago, and in answer to the Chamberlain's incautiously put question on the streets of Berlin after the gypsy woman who had been in Jüterbog the past spring, straightaway pushed herself forward, and under a false name had volunteered for the task he was trying to offer. The horse dealer, noting a strange resemblance between her and his late, lamented wife Lisbeth, such that he felt like asking her if she wasn't by any chance her grandmother—not only her facial features, her hands, which had beautiful bones, and especially her way of gesturing with them, reminded him of her intensely: also a mole that his wife had had on her neck, he saw as well on hers—the horse dealer asked her to sit down, all the while his thoughts whirred in his brain, and asked her what in all the world brought her to him on behalf of the Chamberlain. The woman, while Kohlhaas's old dog sniffed at her, and as she patted his neck, wagged his tail, replied: "The task with which the Chamberlain entrusted her was to tell him the paper's mysterious answers to three vital questions concerning the ruling house of Saxony. To warn him regarding an agent currently in Berlin hoping to seize him. And to ask for the paper on the grounds that it was no longer safe on his person. The real purpose, however, in which she was coming to him, was to tell him that the threat to separate him from the paper by cunning or force was empty and spurious. Under the protection of the Brandenburg Elector, as he presently was, he had nothing to fear for it. Yes, that the paper was far safer on him than it would be on her, and he had best not hand it over to anyone under any pretext. And then she concluded by saying that she thought it prudent for him to make use of the paper for the purpose she had given it to him then at the fair in Jüterbog, to listen to the offer that had been made to him on the frontier by the Freiherr von Stein, and surrender the paper, which was presently of no value to him, to the Saxon Elector in return for life and liberty."

Kohlhaas, jubilant at the power that had been given him to wound his enemy mortally in the heel even as he made to trample him in the dirt, replied: Not for anything in the world, little mother, not for anything. And he squeezed her ancient hand, and asked only what answers did the paper give to the momentous questions? The woman, who by now had picked up Kohlhaas's youngest child where he had been play-ing on the floor and set him on her lap, said: "Maybe not the world, Kohlhaas, horse dealer, but for this pretty little fair-haired boy!" and so saying she laughed at him and pressed him to her and kissed him, while he stared at her with big eyes, and with her wizened hands she gave him an apple that she took from her bag. Kohlhaas remarked in confusion that the children themselves, when they were grown, would praise him for his action, and that he, for them and their children's children, could think of no better course than to keep the paper. He asked furthermore who, given his recent experiences, would insure him against further swindle, and if he wouldn't in the end give up the paper to the Elector to no purpose, just as he had given up his army at Lützen? "Who once breaks his word to me," he said, "I will no longer speak with; and only your certain and unambiguous demand could separate me, good little mother, from the paper through the agency of which, miraculously, everything I have suffered contrives my satisfaction." The woman, setting the infant down on the floor, said that in some respects he was right, and that he should do as he pleased. And with that she took up her crutches and made to leave. Kohlhaas repeated his question concerning the contents of the miraculous paper; he wished, when she replied cursorily, "Then let him open it, even though it were nothing but curiosity," to hear from her about a thousand other matters before she went away; who she was, how she came by the knowledge that was in her, why she had refused the paper to the Elector for whom it was written, and, of all the thousands of other people, given it to him, who had never desired her arcane knowledge?

Now it turned out that at that moment the sound was heard of a few police officers climbing up the stairs; so that the woman, suddenly alarmed at being met with in these rooms, replied: "Farewell, Kohlhaas, farewell. If we should meet again, I will answer all your questions." And then, turning towards the door, she called out: "Farewell, dear little ones, farewell!" and she kissed the little brood in order, and left.

In the meantime, the Saxon Elector, prey to gloomy thoughts, had summoned a couple of astrologers named Oldenholm and Olearius, who at that time enjoyed great fame in Saxony, and consulted them regarding the contents of the mysterious paper and what it portended for himself and his heirs. Since these men, in the course of profound researches made over many days in the castle tower at Dresden were unable to agree whether the prophesy pertained to future centuries or the present date, with perhaps an eye to the crown of Poland, with whom relations were still far from settled, their learned dispute, instead of allaying it served only to exacerbate the unhappy monarch's disturbance, not to say despair, and finally to a degree that was quite intolerable to his spirit. Further, the Chamberlain chose this time to tell his wife, who was on the point of following him to Berlin, to break it to the monarch first how his attempt with an old crone had missed fire, and she had disappeared, along with the hope of acquiring the paper that was in the possession of Kohlhaas, on whom the death sentence had now been passed, and following an exhaustive inspection of the files of the case, signed by the Brandenburg Elector, and the execution date had been set for the Monday after Palm Sunday. On receipt of which news the Elector, his heart torn by distress and regret like that of a man wholly lost, locked himself up in his room for two days, fed up with life, would take no nourishment, and on the third, quite suddenly, with a brief note to the palace, that he was going to Dessau to hunt, left Dresden. Where he was actually headed, and if he actually went somewhere other than Dessau we leave in uncertainty, seeing as the sources from which we have compiled this account quit company at this point and become contradictory. All that can be confirmed is that the Earl of Dessau at this point was incapable of hunting because he was lying ill in bed at his uncle Heinrich's in Braunschweig, and Lady Heloise the following evening arrived in Berlin at her husband the Chamberlain Kunz's in the company of one Count Königstein, who she claimed was a cousin.

In the meantime, at the orders of the Brandenburg Elector, the death sentence had been read to Kohlhaas, his chains were taken off him, and his personal fortune, which had been taken away from him in Dresden, was now restored to him. And since the lawyers who had been sent to him by the court asked him what arrangements he wanted made with his goods and chattels after his death, with the help of a notary he drew up a will leaving everything to his children and named as his executor his honest neighbor at Kohlhaasenbrück. After that, nothing resembled the calm contentment of his final days, because at a special dispensation from the Elector, the doors of the prison in which he was held were thrown open, and all his friends in the city, of whom he had many, were able to visit him day and night. Yes, he even had the satisfaction of having the theologian Jakob Freising, an emissary of Doctor Luther's, enter his cell with a no doubt highly interesting letter, which alas has been lost, and then of receiving Holy Communion at the hands of this gentleman in the presence of two Brandenburg Deans. With that, while the city continued to hope for a reprieve, we were now arrived at the ominous Monday after Palm Sunday, the day on which, following his overly rash attempt to obtain justice, he was to leave the world at peace. Escorted by a numerous guard, with his two sons in his arms (which was a privilege he had expressly asked for from the court), and led by the theologian Jakob Freising, he was just passing through the prison gates, when among a melancholy crowd of acquaintances, pressing his hands and bidding him farewell, the castellan of the Elector's castle stepped up to him, features working, and gave him a piece of paper, delivered to him by an old woman. Kohlhaas looked at the man strangely (he didn't know him well) and opened the sheet of paper, the seal of which, pressed in wax, straightaway reminded him of the old gypsy woman. But who can describe the surprise that came over him when he read the following news: "Kohlhaas, the Saxon Elector is in Berlin; he has gone on ahead to the execution site, and will be known to you, should you so desire, by a hat with white and blue feathers. I have no need to tell you the purpose of his being here; he will have the cartridge dug up as soon as you are cold and in the ground and have the paper that is inside opened.—Your Elisabeth."

Kohlhaas turned to look at the castellan in bewilderment, and asked: did he know the curious woman who gave him the note? But since the castellan replied: "Kohlhaas, the woman—" and stopped in midreply, moved on by the column of people again, he was unable to catch what it was the man said, who was shaking in every limb.

When he reached the execution square, he saw the Elector of Brandenburg with his retinue, among them the Chancellor Heinrich von Geusau, on horseback in an endless mass of people: to his right was the Imperial lawyer Franz Müller, with a copy of the death sentence in his hand; to his left with the verdict of the Dresden Court, his own attorney, Master

Anton Zäuner; a herald in the middle of the half-open circle ringed by the common people, with a bundle of possessions, and the two horses, shining with health, pawing the ground. For Heinrich von Geusau had forced through his suit on his master's behalf in Dresden, point for point, and without the least diminishment against the Junker Wenzel von Tronka, so that the horses, restored to honor by having a flag waved over their heads, and taken back from the knackery which had been looking after them, fed to health by the people of the Junker, and in the presence of a commission specifically formed to that end to confirm the fact, were handed over to his lawyer in the market place at Dresden. Then the Brandenburg Elector spoke, as Kohlhaas, flanked by the guards, climbed up the hill towards him: Now then, Kohlhaas, today's the day when justice will be done unto you. See here, what I have for you, everything you lost at the castle at Tronkenburg, and the restitution of which I, as your ruler owed you: horses, neckerchief, imperial gulden, linens, even the hospital costs for your squire Herse fallen at Mühlheim. Are you satisfied with me?

Kohlhaas read with shining eyes the judgment handed him at a look from the Chancellor, settled the two children he was carrying in his arms down on the ground, and since he also found an item wherein the Junker Wenzel was sentenced to two years in prison, he fell to his knees before the Elector, hands crossed over his chest, quite overcome by feeling. He joyfully assured the Chancellor getting to his feet and laying a hand across his stomach that his deepest wish on earth had been satisfied; he went up to the horses, scrutinized them, patted them on their sturdy necks, and cheerfully declared to the Chancellor in returning: "That they be given to his two sons, Heinrich and Leopold!" The Chancellor, Heinrich von Geusau, looking down at him kindly from on horse-back, promised him on behalf of the Elector that his last wish would be holy to him, and urged him to dispose of the other items in the bundle as he thought fit. Thereupon Kohlhaas called to old mother Herse, whom he had seen among the multitude in the square, and giving the things to her, he said: "Little mother, this is for thee!"—adding the sum he had received in damages as a present to the money in the bundle, for the care and sustenance of her old days.

The Elector called out: "Now, Kohlhaas, horse dealer, you who have enjoyed such satisfaction, prepare yourself to give similar satisfaction to His Imperial Majesty, whose attorney stands here, for the breach of the peace of which you were guilty." Kohlhaas, doffing his hat and throwing it on the ground, said he was prepared! He presented the children, having once more lifted them off the ground and held them in his arms, to his neighbor at Kohlhaasenbrück, and while the latter led them away from the square in silent tears, stepped up to the block. He untied his neckcloth and opened his shirt; when with a glance into the crowd now rather close to him, he spotted between two knights half-obscuring him with their bodies, the familiar man with blue and white feathers on his hat. With a sudden leap that took his guard by surprise, Kohl-haas stepped up to him, ripped the cartridge away from his chest, took out the paper, broke the seal, and read it; and not taking his eyes off the man with the blue and white feathered hat, who was already giving in to the sweetest hopes, put it in his mouth and swallowed it. The man with the blue and white feathered hat fell down in a swoon at the sight, cramp-ing. Kohlhaas, though, while his shaken retainers bent down to their lord and picked him up off the ground, returned to the scaffold, where his head fell under the executioner's ax.

And so endeth the story of Kohlhaas. His body was laid in a coffin to near-universal mourning, and while the bearers took it up to bury it with all solemnity in a cemetery outside town, the Elector summoned the sons of the departed to him and with a word to his Chancellor that they were to be raised in his page school, knighted the pair of them. The Elector of Saxony, torn in body and soul, returned to Dresden, where further developments may be learned elsewhere. Michael Kohlhaas's vigorous and bonny heirs, though, continued to thrive in Mecklenburg as recently as the last century.